Seventeen-year old Mel Calder is desperate for her life to change, and she is learning the hard way that only she can make it happen. Left alone in their run-down house after her mother's breakdown, she decides to repair and redecorate it for her mother when she comes home, but it's not long before the whole neighbourhood is involved.

When Mel meets attractive Mitch Hamilton, lead guitarist with top rock group Assassination, Mitch is more than willing to help with the house, but Mel is suspicious. She has no time for a boyfriend, particularly a famous one, who will be off to other girls in other countries soon enough, and besides there's her lovely teacher, young Mr. Edwards, so helpful and sympathetic. So when Mitch announces his intention to marry Mel, no one is more astounded than Mel herself, except, perhaps, Mitch's girlfriend, the formidable Roxy Leigh...

In her latest compulsively readable novel, Liz Berry has created a courageous and resourceful heroine, who finds she is able to assert her independence and against the odds, make a future for herself.

Liz Berry lives in London. She is a painter who exhibits her work regularly. She has been head of art in an East London high school, a careers guidance counsellor helping young people plan for their futures, worked in politics, and for a well-known examination body. She also runs her own art gallery.

MEL

Liz Berry

Gallery 41 (Books)
London

First published 1988 by Victor Gollancz, London
First paperback edition 1990 Penguin Books, London
US edition published 1991 Viking Penguin, New York

New paperback edition 2006
Gallery 41 (Books)
3 Church End,
London E17 9RJ

ISBN 978-0-954-88646-2
ISBN 0-9548864-6-1

Printed and bound by CPI Antony Rowe, Eastbourne

One

Mel was waiting.

She was sitting on the high brick wall on top of the railway embankment which blocked the end of her street. The evening had drawn in early with its smell of burning wood smoke and its low dark clouds. Late June. But it seemed like autumn.

The drizzle was soaking through her old school blouse and dripping off the ends of her hair. Her hands, clutching the wall, were wet and cold, but she did not notice. She was rigid with tension, watching the last three boys playing football in the narrow space between the dumped, wheel-less cars. Nassim Khan, Kevin Molloy and Stevie Miller. Cowcross Street had a game of football going on every day, all the year, every year. Only the kids changed. She knew they would go in soon. It was getting late. She had chosen her time carefully. She had only to wait; but the waiting was hard now she had made up her mind.

A chill breeze eddied down the street, rolling the dirt and rubbish against the cars. Like the people in the houses, she thought, swept up into the mean, decaying streets, built in the eighteen-nineties by a builder who had brought a gentleman's house in Epping Forest with his handsome profit. Three small streets, jammed in the triangle of waste ground between the street market, the main line to Liverpool Street Station, and the Underground railway, where it came above ground. The houses were falling to pieces. Full of poor people trapped and hating each other. They were never going to get out. The street was a dead end, in all ways. Especially hers. The grim joke pleased her. Her shaking hands tightened on the wall.

Only a little longer to wait, then she would let go and fall backwards on to the live rail in front of the next tube train when it came out of the tunnel.

"There's a kid up the embankment," said Vi Brown's latest boyfriend, knotting his tie at the window of Number Three. "That right? Dangerous, isn't it?"

"A girl?"

He nodded.

"Mel Calder." She got up and stood next to him, staring out into the gloomy dusk. "Lives over the road. Number Six."

"It's raining. She must be soaked. What's she doing?"

"Doesn't want to go home."

"Poor little bugger. She looks a right waif."

"She's treated bad. Father's dead."

"I thought they looked after kids like that now."

"So did I. Maybe they don't know about her. It's been going on for years. I should have done something, I suppose. But there's all this lot—all the so-called respectable ones, like him and her next door, and nosey Flo Hickey on the corner; they don't do a thing."

He shrugged. "Come on, forget it, Vi. Let's get a drink."

"She's there again. That's four times this week," said Mrs Nicholls, next door, peering out between the heavy net curtains of Number Five. "She looks ill. Not even a jacket. Reg, you'll have to do something."

"Such as what?"

"We ought to tell the NSPCC or the Welfare."

"If I ring the Social Services, they'll take her away and put

6

her in a home. Do you think she wants that? She looks after her mother, doesn't she? What will her mother do then? We'll only make it worse. Just mind your own business. We don't want to get involved with any of these people. They won't thank us for interfering."

"It isn't *right!*" said Mr Hussain, in Urdu, to his wife, looking out of the window of Number Eight. "The sound of blows. The cries. Where are her relatives? The family should take care of her. Why isn't someone looking after her?"

"There is no one," said his wife, sighing. "Saira says there is no family, and the mother is sick in the head."

"The authorities should take some action," said Mr Hussain angrily. "I cannot understand why her school has done nothing."

"That Mel Calder is on the wall again," said Mrs Miller, worried, in the end house next to the embankment. "She'll fall down one day. Right on to those electric rails."

"What you want me to do about it, woman?" Mr Miller shook out his Sunday newspaper, irritably. "Is it anything to do with us? She's a white girl. Let her own people do something about it. We got our own troubles." He went on looking at the newspaper, but his eyes had ceased to move, and he was wondering for the hundredth time if there was any way at all to help the girl. The whole street had heard the mother screaming and swearing. It was getting worse.

Mrs Miller glared angrily at him, and went to the front door. Her powerful Caribbean contralto reached the end of the street easily.

"Stevie Miller, you get in here. It's late."

"Aw, Mum. Half an hour . . ."

"*Now.*"

"Ten minutes," he bargained.

"If I have to come after you, boy, you'll be sorry."

Stevie spoke to his friends, collected his football and dribbled it, as slowly as he dared, along the broken pavement. Kevin and Nassim trailed after him disconsolately to their own homes. No ball!

Mrs Miller looked up at the embankment wall. "And you, Mel Calder. Just you get down off that wall and get inside. You'll catch cold sitting there like a fool in the rain!"

Mel roused herself and stared down at Mrs Miller bitterly. Anyone would think she was ten years old, like Stevie, instead of seventeen. She had a right to sit on the wall if she wanted to. She hunched a shoulder and turned her head away.

Mrs Miller went in and slammed the door.

Mel felt a vague regret about upsetting Mrs Miller who had been kind on more than one occasion, inviting her in for ginger beer and cake when Lucinda had been her friend. But it didn't matter now, anyway. Nothing mattered any more.

She moved her shoulders and felt the wet fabric sticking to her bruised back. Nobody cared. The PE staff at school had asked about the bruises once or twice, but had accepted her thin explanations without comment. Nobody really wanted to know. She would die and no one would bother. She wouldn't have to feel anything any more. No more fear and pain and disgust. Nothing was ever going to change. Admit it, and let it all go. When the train came she had only to lift her hands off the wall like this . . . put her legs straight out . . . balance backwards . . . tip a bit more and . . .

The tube train roared out of the tunnel suddenly, before she was ready, and flashed silver towards her.

Mel caught her breath, hung dizzily for a moment, the rattle and crash of the train in her ears, then, of their own accord, her hands clamped to the top of the wall and propelled her forward, away from the train and its dragging slipstream of wind.

She fell awkwardly, scraping her bruised back on the wall,

8

landing clumsily. Her ankle turned and she continued on down the steep embankment in a slide of mud and weeds.

At the bottom, among the rusty prams and old mattresses, she put her head against her knees, trembling, fighting for breath. It was a moment before the realisation hit her. She was still alive. She had failed. *She couldn't do it.* Stupid cowardly bitch. All she had to do was let go. Just *let go.* It would have been over now.

She got up eventually, still trembling, kicking away the old tins and cardboard boxes furiously. Her jeans were covered with mud and leaves. Mechanically she tried to brush them away, but the mess got worse. She eased her wet blouse away from her back and felt a trickle of blood running down. She straightened cautiously and climbed painfully through the bent iron railings. She walked along the little street, trying not to limp on her swelling ankle. She hoped nobody had seen the undignified fall into the heaps of rubbish. Suddenly she wanted to laugh hysterically. So much for the big suicide attempt.

The lights were coming on in the windows, cheerful in the wet dusk. There were six small houses on her side of the road, a terrace, with no front gardens, their narrow doors and windows fronting the pavement. Anybody could look in. The four houses opposite were slightly larger, with bay windows, their doors down the side, and they had small front gardens. Their lights were on too, but Mel walked along, her eyes on the pavement. She did not want to see any scenes of happy family life.

Her own house was in darkness still. As she let herself in with her door key, the smell hit her once again. Damp, drains, stale cooking, pee, *dirt.* Mouldy sourness.

She went down the little passage to the stairs, and then, hesitating, reluctantly turned and opened the living room door. The room was lit only by the flickering blue of the television, but it was a long time since there had been a picture. Her mother was sitting there, silent, blank. Only her hands were moving, tearing a newspaper very carefully into tiny perfect squares which fluttered into a cardboard carton at her feet.

She did not look up, even when Mel turned on the dim centre light. She looked dreadful. Her hair was dirty and matted, her frock stained and smelling. She was skeleton-thin, and her skin was pale grey and flaky. She was thirty-five, but Mel thought she looked at least twenty years older. The room was in its usual indescribable state of confusion and dirt. Mel saw, feeling sick fear, that her mother must have been out again last night, gathering a new supply of newspapers and cardboard cartons from the rubbish people had put out on their doorsteps for the refuse collection. They stood about the room in heaps and piles, mouldy and stinking. Nearly the whole floor space was covered now.

Mel stood in the doorway, defensively. "Do you want any food?"

There was a silence, then her mother twisted her head stiffly and stared at her.

"*Food*. Do you want any?" Mel said again.

"No."

"Then I'm going to bed." She turned away from the empty, staring eyes.

"Mel?"

"What is it?"

There was another silence. Mel turned, reluctantly. The huge dark eyes, so like her own, were wide and begging now. Begging for *something*, but Mel did not know what. Her heart turned over uncomfortably.

"You want something? Some tea?" The tea she had made that morning was still there on the table, untouched. "You ought to have something."

"No."

"Then what is it?"

"Nothing."

The eyes had died again and the newspaper squares went on falling from her thin fingers, like tears.

Mel closed the door behind her and stood against it, feeling ill. What on earth was she going to do? Surely there was somebody somewhere who would help? She turned and walked up the stairs slowly, her shoulders bent, her feet dragging. She was fooling herself. She knew very well that there was no help anywhere.

Two

Sundays were the worst. The weekdays were better.

On the school wall, under the sign *Inner London Education Authority. William Watt Comprehensive School,* some long-ago joker had sprayed the word COLDITZ. Mel knew that many of her fellow pupils felt school was like a prison camp or a torture chamber, but they were the lucky ones who had somewhere better to go and something better to do. For a few, including Mel, it was a refuge.

On Monday morning it was a relief to push through the glass doors into the cheerful noisy chaos, sniffing the harsh, clean smell of disinfectant on vinyl tiles. Over the years she had trained herself to concentrate on her school work, no matter what happened at home, finding to her surprise that she actually enjoyed it, enjoyed getting good results, enjoyed stretching her brain. After school she stayed on to play badminton, joined the drama group and the sewing club, ran discos and helped Home Economics cater for the PTA's frequent bingo sessions and other fund-raising activities. She would do anything, in fact, that kept her from going home until the last possible moment. But the summer holidays would start soon, and the school would be closed.

Mel stared out of the window. The art room was at the top of the building, its huge windows giving spectacular views of a red and black rooftop mosaic patched with green trees. Row upon row of buildings, all shapes and sizes, crushed together, stretching away as far as the eye could see to the heat haze on the horizon. Six interminable weeks trapped in Cowcross Street. She did not think that she would be able to stand it this year. Her pencil, moving over the drawing paper, stopped, as she thought again of the embankment wall.

"Mel!" shouted Keith Edwards, her new young art teacher, across the room. "Mrs Green wants to see you."

He came and looked over her shoulder at her drawing of two crumbling houses. "That's really good. I like that detail of the broken plaster and the smashed windows."

"The people are awful though."

"Mmm. A bit stiff. Where are these buildings?"

"Just down there. You can see them. I pass them on my way home."

"You've got a nice little sketch there. Looks like you've got a feeling for architecture. You might think of doing something about houses for your Special Study theme, if you haven't chosen anything else, that is."

"Not yet. I'm not thinking very well just now."

She had given up Art in the Third Year in favour of more academic subjects. It had seemed a good idea to pick it up again in the Sixth, to get an easy extra exam pass, along with her A levels in English Literature, French and History, but it was proving more difficult and more absorbing than she had thought.

"Who did you say wanted me?"

"Mrs Green. Don't go in your art shirt."

Mel grinned, but her heart had started to bang unpleasantly. Something serious. Everyone knew that Mrs Green, the pernickety Deputy Head, dealt with the most important matters in the school, while the Head played with the timetable boards and school governors.

By the time she reached Mrs Green's office, her sense of foreboding was acute, and she felt physically sick. There was a visitor sitting in the armchair across from Mrs Green's desk, a tall young woman with a cheerful, freckled face and a halo of frizzy red hair.

Mrs Green said, "Mel, this is Miss Tracey from the Social Services Department."

"Hello, Mel." Her voice was too sympathetic, too professionally cheerful, like a doctor's. Mel stiffened. She saw that under the jolly smile, Miss Tracey was watching her carefully, and that the smile had not reached her eyes.

"Come and sit down, lovey." She patted the chair next to her. "You can call me Dee if you like."

Mel did not move. She said, stiffly, "What is it? What's happened?"

Dee Tracey stopped smiling. "We have some rather bad news for you, I'm afraid, lovey. Your mother . . ."

The sense of impending disaster broke over Mel. *Suicide*, she thought. *She's committed suicide.* Briefly, the room swung darkly.

Mrs Green's cool voice penetrated, discouraging hysteria. "*Sit down*, Mel. It's all right. She's not dead. She's been taken to hospital."

"Hob's Green, the hospital for mentally disturbed patients," Dee Tracey said quickly. "Sorry about that, Mel. I didn't mean to give you a fright."

"But I don't understand." Mel drew a deep breath and tried to steady her voice. "She was all right when I left this morning. That is . . . I mean, she was just as usual. I know she's ill but . . ."

"Yes, well, very ill, I'm afraid. She's had what's called a mental breakdown, and it is rather serious." She sounded as though she was explaining to a child, Mel thought angrily. As if she didn't know what was wrong with her mother. "She should have been seeing a doctor regularly," Dee Tracey went on, kindly. "She might have been okay with tablets. But of course, you weren't to know that."

14

Tablets, thought Mel, bitterly, remembering her mother's hysterical screaming when she had said she was going to make the doctor come. "They'll take me away! Put me in an asylum. Your own mother. You want to get rid of me. You're trying to kill me . . ." She had leapt at Mel, clawing, screaming, and Mel had fled to her refuge on top of the embankment wall, creeping back very late when she knew her mother would be in bed. The next morning her mother had been passive again, dazed, and Mel had made sandwiches and tea before going to school. But she had begun to wedge her bedroom door at night as the temper attacks grew more violent.

"Anyway, you'll be able to visit her in the hospital soon. In the meantime we have to get you fixed up, so if you'll get your coat and things, we'll be on our way." Dee Tracey closed the folder on her lap, and got to her feet, smoothing her narrow black skirt down her thighs. Her long oval fingernails were the same dark orange as her lipstick. Mel felt rumpled and grubby. "But where are we going? What's happening? I don't understand."

"Your aunt down in Stockwell. You'll have to stay there until your mother comes out of hospital. And we have to fix you up with a new school today."

"My *mother's* aunt," said Mel, automatically. Great Aunt Edie, who spat in the sink and smelled of diarrhoea. She had stayed there three years ago. "How long will my mother be in hospital?"

"Not long we hope." Dee Tracey smiled encouragingly. She had large white teeth. Like a chimpanzee, Mel thought, resentfully.

"One week? Two weeks? A month?"

"Perhaps a little longer than that."

"Six months?"

Neither of the two women would meet Mel's eyes.

"Well, as I said, lovey, it is a serious breakdown. It all

15

depends on how she responds to treatment. This is her second breakdown after all."

Mrs Green said, "Now, if you'll just go and get your coat . . ."

"No," said Mel. Feeling had begun to come back and with it a growing anger. They were trying to push her around. "No!" she said again, her voice hardening. "First, I want to know exactly what happened to my mother."

"You know your mother is mentally ill, lovey. What else is there to say? One of your neighbours, Mrs Miller, phoned for an ambulance. Your mother was running up and down the road in her nightdress, crying and shouting."

Mel, ashen, said, "I want to see her."

"There's no point at the moment, lovey. She won't know you. She got violent. Several people had to hold her down. It's a pity you didn't think to get a doctor to her before it got so bad. It must have been very difficult for you though. You could have come to us, you know. There's all kinds of help available. We could have provided support, a family case-worker maybe, a health visitor, a home help to clear up all that mess in the house . . ."

"You say that *now*," said Mel, the anger and bitterness choking her throat, "but you didn't help. You did *nothing! Nobody* helped."

"You've had a rather bad time, Mel," said Mrs Green, soothingly. "But you must put it all behind you now. Once you're with your aunt in Stockwell . . ."

"*No,*" said Mel. She could feel her voice rising out of her control. "I'm not going to Great Aunt Edie's. She hates having me. And I'm not changing schools in the middle of my A levels and mucking up my chances of passing."

Dee Tracey said doubtfully, "Well, I suppose you could stay in your own home. But the conditions . . . I mean, it's not exactly . . ." She glanced at Mrs Green.

"You need someone to look after you, Mel," said Mrs Green, coming to the rescue.

But Mel had seen the significant look and felt the blood burning her cheeks. She stared at Dee Tracey. Patronising, conceited cow, with her silly Sloane Ranger voice. *Lovey.* What did she know of the way people like Mel had to live?

"Who do you think has looked after me for the last three years?" She sucked in thin streams of air as the fury blocked her throat again. "I'm not a little girl. I'm seventeen. I do the cleaning, the washing, the cooking, the shopping. I handle the money. My mother hasn't cooked a meal in two years. She didn't know what time of the day or night it was. She didn't know if I was in or out or dead or alive. And she didn't care. And nobody else did either, *lovey.*"

"I'm sure you coped fantastically well, but . . ."

"Can't you put me in a foster home? Find me a place in a hostel?"

"Take you into Care, you mean? Oh, there's no need for that Mel. We hardly ever take Care proceedings for seventeen-year-olds. Not unless there are reasons to think they are in moral or physical danger. Believe me, in this area we aren't looking for problems. The whole of the social services are stretched to breaking point. There aren't enough foster homes anyway, or hostel places. We assume that if you are seventeen you are capable of looking after yourself—as you just said. The only thing is, you might be a bit lonely all by yourself in the house, so that's why I think you'd be well advised to go to your auntie. Sorry, your *great* aunt."

Mel stared at her disbelievingly. They were still not going to help her. Even now, when almost the worst disaster of her life had struck, they *still* weren't going to do anything. No foster parents. No hostel. The lovely dream, which she had hardly acknowledged even to herself, of the clean, suburban home with fitted carpets and flower-printed duvets, the friendly jokey foster dad, and an understanding mum who would cuddle her sometimes when she felt low, that lovely impossible dream, faded away, leaving harsh, gritty, real life.

She felt sick. Great Aunt Edie again with her dark, furry teeth, and disgusting, rumbling cough.

All this time they had ignored her, let her struggle on without raising a finger to help. She had always imagined that help must come one day. The doctor, or someone at school, would notice the bruises maybe, and see she was looked after. But nobody was going to help her. Nobody cared. Although she had told herself so many times, deep down she had never really believed it. But now, suddenly, she felt she had stepped on a ladder rung which was not there and plunged off into empty space, falling, with the dark abyss opening all around her. For a moment she hung there, then a flood of wild fury poured through her.

She jumped to her feet and stared at them accusingly, hiding her clenched hands against her sides. "You're not going to help me at all, are you? I'm just a nuisance. Not a person—a *problem*. Something to tidy away like a dirty crisp bag in the playground."

"Now then, Mel," said Mrs Green, disapprovingly. "There's no need for all the high drama. You're usually such a sensible girl. And you did well by your mother."

"Not well enough," said Mel, bitterly. "Miss Tracey said so, didn't she? I didn't get the doctor. I didn't keep the place clean. I didn't get all the marvellous help she says is available . . . It's all my fault my mother's raving mad, isn't it? *Isn't it?*"

Dee Tracey was appalled. "Oh no, Mel, that's not at all what I . . ."

"Well, let me tell you, Miss Tracey," Mel spat the words. "I went to the doctor—my mother wouldn't take the tablets. I was trying to poison her, wasn't I? And I tried to get help from the Social Services. *Your* office, Miss Tracey. You know

18

what they said? 'It's a medical problem. Get the doctor to her.' No help. No home help. No family caseworker. *Nothing.* The doctor said she'd have to go to the surgery in person, but she wouldn't go. And all the time she was having these violent attacks. *Nobody wanted to know!"*

"That's enough, Mel." Mrs Green got up briskly, and patted Mel's shoulder. "You've had a hard time. No one is blaming you for anything. You aren't responsible for your mother's illness. You tried to do your best. Now go and wait outside for a few minutes. Miss Tracey and I will try to sort something out."

Mel's control began to go. She tried to breathe deeply, but her voice was shaking. "I never realised. One day, I thought, someone will see. They'll start to look after us and it will be all right." Her voice broke. "Well, today I realised. Nobody really cares. You only have yourself." She took a long shuddering breath. "Well, *all right*, Miss Tracey, Mrs Green. I'm not stupid. I've learned my lesson. From now on I'm taking care of myself. No more waiting for help to show up. No more waiting for a fairy godmother. Now get this. You are not tidying *me* away to Great Aunt Edie. You're not ruining my chance of a decent future. I'm finishing my A levels *here* and I'll stay in my own place and look after myself!"

She wrenched open the door and turned back. "And you two—you can piss off!"

She spun around and bounced off a solid, immovable body standing just outside the door.

"What kind of language is that, Mel Calder?" asked Mrs Miller, sternly.

Mel glared at her wildly, incredulous. *Mrs Miller again?* She must get away, already her legs were buckling under her. She tried to push past, but Mrs Miller was gripping her shoulders firmly, comfortingly, holding her up.

"There, there, baby," said Mrs Miller. "Everything is

going to be all right. Everything is coming right now. You'll see . . ." She folded Mel closer, holding her head against her shoulder, rocking her rhythmically. Mel stopped struggling and quieted, like an animal gentling under careful hands. For a moment she was tempted to surrender, to cling and howl childishly, begging for comfort. She made a supreme effort, pulled herself away and stumbled to a chair.

She turned her back on them all, humiliated and ashamed. She had lost control so badly. All her dignity gone, screaming and raving like a lunatic. A wave of horror brought the perspiration out on her forehead. Screaming and raving *like her mother*. Was she going mad too?

Mrs Miller said, "What is going on here?"

Mrs Green smiled. "The Secretary's office is next door. I'm afraid you've come to the wrong room, Mrs . . . er . . ."

"Miller. You know me, Mrs Green, I have had three children in this school. My son Ben is in the fifth form. But today I have come about Mel. It looks as though I have arrived just in time." She trod forward purposefully and closed the door behind her. "I am not at all happy at the way this business has been handled."

Dee Tracey coloured. "Mel is a little upset. Her mother . . ."

"I know all about her mother," said Mrs Miller. "More, I think, than those who *ought* to know. We meet again, Miss Tracey. I am the neighbour in Cowcross Street who sent for the doctor, the police and the social services this morning. I stayed with Mrs Calder and packed some things for her. Now I am concerned with Mel."

"Yes, I'm sorry I didn't recognise you," said Dee Tracey. "We are all concerned about Mel, Mrs Miller, but we have a little problem. We are trying to persuade her to go to her aunt."

"No problem," said Mrs Miller, firmly. "Mel can come to us. Just across the road at Number Seven. I have a spare room since my daughter got married last year. That's what I came to say."

"Yes, but . . . well . . . I mean, it's not as easy as that."

"We are respectable people. You can make inquiries. I am a Ward Sister at St Joseph's Hospital, and my husband is in the building trade. I have fostered two babies for the Social Services. I have known Mel since she was eleven years old. We would look after her properly."

"I can look after myself," said Mel, angrily.

"I know that," said Mrs Miller. "I have seen that over the years. You can think of yourself as a lodger. A paying guest. You'd rather go to your great auntie like last time?"

Mel swallowed. "You know I wouldn't. I'd rather stay with you." She hesitated and then said, awkwardly, "Thanks."

"That's all right," said Mrs Miller, dryly. "Nobody's expecting you to fall over yourself with gratitude."

Mel flushed. "Look, I'm sorry. I know you're always trying to help me, and I'm grateful, honestly. It's just that . . ."

"It's so long since anybody helped, that you've forgotten how to say 'thank you' properly."

"The thing is," said Dee Tracey quickly, apologetically, "we try to arrange that children should stay with people of their own ethnic group . . ."

Mrs Miller snorted. "White folks foster Black babies. This is a Black family helping a white girl. You have a white foster family for Mel?"

"Well, no, I'm afraid not. But there's her aunt."

"I'm not going there," said Mel, standing up.

"Mel's great auntie is not a suitable person to foster a teenager," said Mrs Miller, uncompromisingly. "I have brought up four children and fostered two babies. You going to give me trouble, Miss Tracey?"

"Well, I'll see if . . ."

21

"I'm a busy woman," said Mrs Miller. "Get it fixed before I find it necessary to have a word with Mr Patel of the Community Relations Council."

Dee Tracey said hastily, "Naturally we are very grateful to you for coming to the rescue, Mrs Miller. I'm sure we can come to an arrangement."

Mrs Miller laughed richly. "That's what I thought, queenie."

"I think we ought to have Mel's Group Tutor in on our discussion," said Mrs Green. "We are rather proud of our pastoral care in this school. Who is your Tutor, Mel?"

"Mr Edwards. But I don't want everyone to know about my mo . . ."

Mrs Green had already picked up her telephone. "If you'll just wait outside for a few minutes, Mel."

Without another word Mel walked out of the room and sat huddled in the waiting area outside, icy cold, now the panic and anger had gone. She stared blindly at the anti-smoking posters on the wall. The voices rose and fell, clearly audible behind the flimsy partition, deciding her future. She didn't care. If it suited her she would go along with them. But she was on her own now, looking after herself.

After a while Keith Edwards came along, looking irritable. "I've been summoned to the Presence. Doesn't she know I've got 5E up there with that idiot Ben Miller larking about, dropping his woolly hat into the paste bucket? What have you been up to Mel?"

Mel went red. "Nothing."

"What am I doing here then?"

"I'm in your tutor group. There's a social worker here . . ." She forced herself to go on, her voice hard. "My mother went mad this morning."

He ran his fingers wearily through his short fair hair. "Oh God. More work. It never rains but it pours."

Mel turned her head away, but not quickly enough and he

22

saw a single tear escape and run down her cheek. She wiped it away with the back of her hand. He felt some compunction, and slid his arm round her, patting her awkwardly. "Don't cry, Mel."

Another tear followed the first. "I'm not," she choked.

"That's right. You're a big girl now."

That was true. He felt the soft curves of her body against him, and stopped feeling like a father and a teacher. He moved away hastily, horrified. Just in time. Mrs Green opened the door.

"We've been waiting for you, Mr Edwards. Miss Tracey, this is Mel's Group Tutor. He's responsible for her progress and welfare here in school. You will be dealing with him rather than myself in future."

Keith Edwards nearly groaned aloud. The Bitch. Buck-passing. As if he didn't have enough work to do in his first year of teaching, without all this so-called pastoral care garbage. He smiled insincerely, charmingly, at Dee Tracey, and went forward to shake her hand. Mrs Green closed the door again.

Mel went and looked out of the window which overlooked the street. An old man hobbled along holding the railings of the school. What would he do when he ran out of railings?

She thought of her mother. The narrow face and demented eyes were there in her head all the time. Now, too late, Mel knew what her mother had been asking for last night. Help. Care. *Love.*

Everybody was asking and nobody was getting or offering.

Except Mrs Miller, insisted her mind, inconveniently. Okay, except Mrs Miller.

The old man had reached the end of the railings. Mel watched, tensely, as though it was an omen. He paused, straightened, took a deep breath, and moved on cautiously, making slow progress along the street.

Mel's shoulders relaxed. She had tried to look after her

mother, hadn't she? Tried to do her best. *Tried.* No marks for trying. There was only right or wrong and she had been wrong. She *was* to blame, whatever Mrs Green said. She ought to have done more, *cared* more. Surely there was some way she could make it up to her mother? Like, take a bunch of flowers to the hospital, her mind sneered cynically.

There must be something she could do, she thought desperately, some real way of helping. Some real way of shifting the heavy guilt which had settled over her heart like a lead blanket. Surely it wasn't too late?

Three

As Mel came out of the school gate at the end of the afternoon, a car hooted behind her. Keith Edwards put his head out of the window, smiling.

"Give you a lift home, Mel."

She hesitated, blushing, aware of the other girls staring enviously at her. "It's all right, Mr Edwards."

He leaned over and swung open the door. "Come on."

"Honestly . . ."

"Don't argue. Dee Tracey's orders. She asked me to take you home this afternoon. See that everything was okay in the house."

She got in reluctantly. She didn't want him to see her home. She didn't want anyone to see it until she could clean it up a bit first. But there was no escape, and when they reached Cowcross Street he parked the car outside Number Six and came in with her.

The tiny passage was dark, the big-patterned wallpaper brown with age, torn and greasy where people had rubbed against it for countless years. There was a narrow piece of lino down the centre of the floor, its pattern worn away, and the stairs were bare wood. To the right were two peeling dark brown doors. The kitchen was straight ahead.

Mel, her face stiff, opened the farthest door.

"You might as well see the worst. This is the living room. This is where she is most of the time. I use the kitchen."

25

The room was small, filled with heavy old furniture—a table, upright chairs, a sideboard. Large cardboard cartons and bundles of newspapers covered every available surface and stood in teetering piles on the floor, leaving only a narrow path from the door to the table.

"It's terrible, isn't it? And it stinks." Mel shivered. The television was still flickering. She went across and turned it off.

Keith looked around, trying not to let Mel see how shaken and appalled he was. The smell made him want to gag.

"What are all these boxes?"

"Take a look."

He flicked open one on the table and stared at the heaped newspaper squares, letting them run through his fingers. "I don't understand."

"That's what she does all day. Packing. That's what she says. Packing." She laughed but the laugh cracked horribly in the middle. "Let's go in the kitchen. It's better there. She wouldn't let me clean in here."

The kitchen was a glass-roofed extension. There was a dark brown dresser built into one wall, a wooden table, an old sink and a gas cooker. They were all clean, smelling overpoweringly of bleach, but even the bleach could not disguise the smell of decay. He saw that there were great damp patches on the walls.

"The rain comes in through the roof," Mel said.

"Who owns it?"

"It used to be a private landlord, but the Council took it over last year. I'm sorry about the smell. Most of it is from the boxes and newspapers she brings in, and the windows don't open." She tried to laugh again. "I'm always frightened the smell will stick to me. It's difficult to keep yourself clean in a kitchen sink."

"There's no bathroom?" He sounded incredulous.

"No, but I wash down twice a day in the kitchen," she said

defensively. "If you can smell anything, it's my clothes. Even though I'm always washing them I can't seem to . . ."

"Mel, you don't *smell!*" He was horrified and embarrassed.

"A lot of people round here do. They can't help it. I don't like to get too close to people in case they can smell me."

He sat down on the wooden kitchen chair and looked around. A battlefield. A constant battle against decay and dirt. Before today he had hardly been aware of Mel's existence. She was so quiet and self-contained, her smooth brown hair pulled back tightly into an elastic band. He understood now why she had always looked scrubbed, shining clean. Her clothes were old, but neatly mended and clean. Just a kid. He hadn't even noticed those fantastic dark eyes.

"I've not had friends for a long time. In case they wanted to come home."

"How did it happen, Mel?"

Mel shrugged and turned away. She filled a kettle under the tap and began to make tea automatically. "I don't know. She was all right when we lived in Lothian, I think. I can't remember very well. I was eleven. My dad was an engineer and we had this nice clean, modern house with carpets and new furniture and a proper kitchen and bathroom. Everything was clean and sparkling . . ."

"Like a TV ad," said Keith, sarcastic.

She stared at him. "What's wrong with that?"

"Even the people are packaged and sterilised for germs."

She thought it over. "Maybe. But if you lived in a street like this you'd be glad of a bit of cleanliness. Lothian seems like a dream now.

"My mother used to get depressed sometimes. But my dad was great. He was big and cheerful. He had fair hair and blue eyes. You look a bit like him actually." She turned hastily away to pour out the tea. "He'd say, 'Buck up, Lovely, we're going out on the town tonight!' And we'd go to a film and

27

have a Chinese meal afterwards. Or he'd take her off to buy a new dress and she'd be okay again.

"She was very pretty then, had her hair done nicely and used to put on make-up. I thought she was wonderful." She laughed bitterly. "You wouldn't recognise her now. She's like a skeleton. Dirty. Hair hanging all over the place and her eyes . . ." She swallowed.

Keith said hastily, "What happened?"

"My dad got killed in an accident at work. A girder fell on him and crushed his ribs. He wasn't insured and the house was mortgaged, so we didn't have any money."

"Didn't the firm pay compensation?"

"I don't think so. My mother was hysterical nearly all the time. Some men came and she signed papers. I suppose they were lawyers. She was crying all the time and all she could think of was to sell the house and move back to London where she came from. Then we moved to Cowcross Street."

Mel stopped, remembering. "We never thought . . . never *imagined* it would be as bad as it was. Her aunt got it for us. It was supposed to be furnished, so we sold all our own furniture.

"The funny thing was, at first the shock of the house was good for her. She stopped crying. She kept telling me not to worry, we'd be moving again pretty quickly, just as soon as she could find somewhere. She wouldn't unpack or do anything to the place because we were going to move soon, you see. Always it was only going to be for a few more weeks."

She looked at Keith, suddenly struck. "You know, everybody who lives in this street is like that. They all hate it. They all think they're only here temporarily and they're going to move out *soon*—so what's the point of doing anything?

"Anyway, my mother got a job in a canteen in a factory and she really worked hard, trying to save. She got more and more tired, you could see, working long hours. 'Don't worry,' she said, at first, 'We won't be staying *here*.' Then she had flu and didn't go back to work. She wouldn't go out at all. Just sat at home looking at the television, or rather, *not* looking. She drank tea and smoked all day, and then she wouldn't even get up from her bed. They took her to the mental hospital for about a month. I had to stay with Great Aunt Edie. That was three years ago."

There was a long silence.

Keith said, "Go on, Mel. Tell me the worst bit."

"When she came back I suggested we might make the house more comfortable, but she said it was all right for the time being and that she wasn't going to throw good money after bad. She got a job in an office, but they closed down after a few months and then she had a lot of odd jobs, a few weeks here and there. Then she'd have a row with someone and walk out or they'd sack her. The hospital gave her these tablets, so she wasn't too depressed, but her temper got worse and worse. You couldn't talk to her at all without being shouted at. Nag, nag, nag, for nothing at all.

"It was like that for maybe two years. And then she didn't do any more work at all. And she didn't go to the hospital and she wouldn't take the tablets. She just sat watching television all day. And then . . ."

Mel took a deep breath. "And then she started going out at night and bringing back cardboard cartons that people put out for the dustmen. And she got piles of newspapers. And started tearing them up . . . *Packing*, she said. We were going to move. I made her go to the doctor. Kept on. Until she went. I don't know what she told him. He gave her valium tablets."

She stopped and swallowed. "Now she won't wash or look after herself. When I try to throw the boxes out she has these mad tempers. And they're getting worse. I didn't know what to do. I told the doctor, but he just gave me repeat prescriptions for valium, which she won't take. He never comes to see."

She burst out, suddenly, "I don't know what else I could have done . . . I know Miss Tracey thought it was my fault, but . . ."

"Now come on, Mel, I'm sure she didn't say that. You know it's not your fault. You've done everything you could."

"It wasn't enough. There *must* have been something else. Miss Tracey said there were all these services, people to help. *But how could I know?* They don't *tell* you. You can't find out."

Keith moved uncomfortably at the anguish in her voice. "Look Mel, there's no point in tearing yourself apart. What's done is done. You've got to forget all that and think about the future."

Mel looked at him, stunned. *Forget it?* Forget all that fear and disgust, the pain and degradation and misery? Almost six years of it? She knew she would never forget. There were lessons there. The hardest she had ever learned. But how could someone as sunny and happy as Keith Edwards ever understand?

She traced the pattern of the worn lino with her foot. "I was stupid. I ought to have found out about things. I ought to have asked someone at school. But I didn't want them to know. I kept waiting for other people to do something. A fairy godmother! I didn't see you had to do things for yourself. That you can't rely on anybody." She tried to laugh. "Just call me Cinders!"

She looked at him directly. "I hate her, Keith. I've hated my mother for two years. I've never admitted that to anyone before. Not even to myself. It was the nagging and shouting. When she began hitting me I thought I'd let her stew in her own juice. I suppose that's why I feel so bad now. I didn't love her enough."

Keith Edwards looked away. He felt inadequate and out of his depth emotionally. He wanted to get away from the deep feelings and the gloom and misery. He slid off the table and stood up. "It's getting late. I'll have to go."

"But please, Keith, what can I *do*? I want to do something for her. Something to make up for it. Tell me what I ought to *do*."

He had no idea. "Calm down, Mel. There's no point in crying." He cast about in his mind for an idea, desperate to get away.

"You can get rid of all those boxes for a start. Now's your chance, before she comes back. And you can clean up. That'll make you feel better. Maybe you could give the living room a coat of paint? It's not difficult if you use emulsion. It would brighten it up and you've got all the summer holidays . . ."

Suddenly, as he was speaking, the idea came to her, complete and beautiful.

"Keith—my special art study. You said we could do it on anything. Could I do it on house decorating? You know, you see those pictures in magazines? 'Before' and 'After'. I could take some photographs and develop them in the dark room with Miss Leslie. And I could write about choosing the colours and find out about painting and decorating. Write about the difficulties. A kind of diary maybe."

He said, puzzled, "I don't see why you shouldn't do an interior design project, but what's that got to do with . . ."

"Don't you see?" Her dark eyes were shining and brilliant. "I want to find out how to make this place look good. Not just *clean*, but comfortable and beautiful. *A surprise*. Then perhaps if she comes back to a nice place she won't get ill again. She could have her friends here and . . ."

He glanced around dubiously, wondering how she expected to turn this stinking dump into anything that could be lived in.

"Where will you get the money?"

"Miss Tracey said she would arrange about Social Security for me. Maybe I can get a Saturday job. I've tried to put something away each week for emergencies, so there's a few pounds there. It might not cost a lot. The paint. Just nice colours."

"You could try, I suppose, though I don't see how it'd help your exams."

"You said I had a feeling for houses. I could do some sketches of the rooms, and show how they would look with different wallpapers and colours. Examples of fabrics. That kind of thing."

He watched her curiously. He had never seen her looking so alive and excited. He realised how serious she was usually. No wonder he had never noticed those fantastic eyes before. Or that body. He looked her over covertly. There was colour in her cheeks. It deepened as she noticed the way he was looking at her.

She said, stammering, "C-could I borrow a camera from the Art Department?"

"Sure. You'll need some film too, and a loose-leaf folder. Drawing paper. I expect you'll want to get going in the holidays."

She nodded, but she meant to start immediately, *tonight*, after he had gone. She went with him to the door. He stood on the doorstep, the evening sun making a halo around his fair hair, and smiled into her eyes.

"Any problems—come to me. Right?"

"Yes."

"I've got a flat the other side of the main road next to the park. Number 27A Highcroft Drive. It's not far. About seven minutes on foot."

Seven minutes. Another world. Mel said, "I know where you live, Mr Edwards."

He grinned and lifted an eyebrow. She blushed scarlet. All

the girls in the school knew where he lived, but she was not about to tell him *that*.

"Call on me for anything, any time, Mel. I really mean that. You can rely on me. I'll help with the project too when you're ready. Come if you need me. *Promise?*"

"I promise. But I'll only come round if it's something really important, Keith—Mr Edwards."

He smiled again. "You've been calling me Keith. That's fine."

Mel's flush deepened. He laughed and brushed her cheek casually with a long finger, and got into his rusty old Ford. Mel watched him go. She had always liked him, he was so helpful and good-tempered. She liked watching him move around the art room, making jokes, his fair hair curling flat against his neck, his tanned hands moving a pencil carelessly over the paper. And today he had put his arm round her, comforted her. Her heart began to thump at the memory. It wasn't possible that he could be interested in her, but she had understood that assessing look he had given her. Suddenly, despite her mother's breakdown, and all the horrors of the day, she felt good.

She was still looking after him dreamily, feeling his touch on her cheek, when a voice next to her said, "Mmm, mmmm! Who's *he*?"

Lucinda Miller. Mel did not meet her eyes, not wanting to start blushing again. Lucinda was uncomfortably sharp.

"My Group Tutor, Keith Edwards."

"Dishy. Very dishy. Not a day over twenty-two, I daresay. Why didn't I get someone like that when I was at William Watt, instead of old Marshmallow, always on about AIDS and Drug Abuse?"

"He came at Easter. You should have stayed on."

"You've got to be joking."

Lucinda, once Mel's best friend, *only* friend, she thought

33

sometimes, had left school last June with eight good exam passes to Mel's five. They did not see each other much now, and when they did, there didn't seem much to talk about.

Mel said, to change the subject, "Finished work?"

"Got off early from the shop. I'm going to Donnelly's tonight. Come over and see what I got to wear. I'll have to put a coat over it in case my Mum sees." She laughed. "I look really good."

"You look good in everything," Mel said, smiling. Lucinda was wearing baggy khaki pants and a strange, mis-shapen orange vest, which glowed against her dark, golden brown skin. She looked fabulous. Her plaited hair was heaped into a fantastic arrangement with orange and green satin ribbons. Only Lucinda had enough confidence to go out looking like that in Cowcross Street and get away with it. She was tall, moving arrogantly like a queen.

"Where did you get that vest?" Mel asked, curious.

"Dr Barnardo's. Fifty pence. Pants and vest. I dyed them."

Mel sighed, conscious of her crumpled school blouse, wishing she had more fashion sense, wishing she had Lucinda's flair and confidence. Keith Edwards might look twice at her then. Suddenly she wished that Lucinda hadn't drifted so far from her, and that they could talk to each other as they used to do. She'd like to ask her advice about Keith Edwards. But they were a long way apart now. It wasn't just the clothes. Lucinda was leaving her behind.

She said, wistfully, "Why don't you come in for a bit?"

Lucinda shook her head. "No time. I came over to get you. The evening meal's ready. I hear they took your mum to the funny house today."

Mel nodded, not wanting to talk about it.

"It's the best thing, Mel. She'll get well there. Mum says you're dossing down in our spare room."

Mel nodded hesitantly, "Your mum came into school.

34

Saved me from Great Aunt Edie. Is it all right? I mean, I don't want you to feel I'm . . . like . . . pushing in."

Lucinda laughed and put her arm round Mel's shoulders. "Welcome to the family. You're a funny colour, but I promise I'll love you like a sister!" She grinned. "Come on now. Grab your nightie and toothbrush, or she'll kill us both."

Mel said, worried, "I've got to talk to your mother about paying for my room and board."

Lucinda laughed again. "Sooner you than me. She'll blast your ears."

"I'm going to pay my way," Mel said, with determination. "No charity. From now on I'm going to run my own life the way I want it."

"Sounds like a Declaration of Independence."

"Yes," said Mel, grimly. "I think you could say that."

Four

Mrs Miller ran her house like an annexe of her ward in St Joseph's. The shining furniture marched with military precision along the walls, leaving the centre of the room to the swirling glory of the rust, brown and yellow carpet. It was Mrs Miller's pride and joy, and she vacuumed it lovingly every day. She had a fine collection of pot plants, but ornaments, litter, smoking, and especially *dust*, were not allowed. Coats must be hung up on the hall pegs. School bags and books must be kept in bedrooms.

The Millers had the end house in Cowcross Street, next to the railway embankment. It was larger than Mel's, with four bedrooms, but only Ben and young Stevie, who shared a room, and Lucinda, were at home now that Mrs Miller's elder daughter Michelle had married. Mr Miller was a carpenter whose work took him all over London. He went out very early in the morning and was hardly ever home before eight at night. He was a quiet man, soft-spoken. He left all the family organisation to his wife, but Mel noticed that when he gave his opinion, Mrs Miller listened.

Everybody, except Mr Miller, was expected to make their beds, keep their rooms clean and do as they were told. There was also a rota of cleaning and household chores, allocated on a strictly fair, non-sexist basis, and even Lucinda didn't try to duck out. Mel joined in willingly, glad to be doing something that made her feel part of the family.

She had settled down well. It was luxury to have proper

meals cooked for her, and strange going to sleep with a lot of other people in the house. She had the small boxroom at the back, with a comfortable bed, a cupboard for hanging clothes and a dressing table. Mrs Miller had given her a door key and told her she was free to come and go as she pleased, but she was expected to be on time for the evening meal and in by eleven. No late night parties, no discos or clubs without notice.

"Parties! I'm not popular like Lucinda," Mel laughed wryly. "I've never even had a boyfriend. I'll be over the road most of the time cleaning up and decorating." She had told Mrs Miller all about her idea for surprising her mother.

"I'm going to clear away all the bad things of the past, so we can start again. I want to have it all done by the time she comes out of hospital."

"There's plenty of time," said Mrs Miller. "Don't kill yourself." Privately she thought Mel would have much more time than she imagined.

Mel had been to see her mother and thought she looked better now they had cleaned her up.

"She was just sitting there. She didn't say anything. She was just staring blankly. I suppose they're giving her some sort of treatment."

"Drugs," said Mrs Miller, shaking out fluffy rice into a dish. "That's to calm her. Don't expect miracles, Mel. Recovery from a breakdown is a long business."

Mel watched her. Mrs Miller was a nurse and probably knew just how bad her mother was. "They said it would be best to go in every fortnight."

Mrs Miller nodded. "Give her a chance to adjust."

"I hate the place. There's this bright day room, modern, a lot of colour, and all these worn, tired people hardly moving. Living dead."

"They'll get better," said Mrs Miller. "Most of them. Some of them."

37

"How do you stand it?" asked Mel. "Nursing, I mean."

"It's a job. You've got to have a job. If you have to do something, you learn how to do it—and then do it. You'll see."

A week later Dee Tracey called in, and after a private word with Mrs Miller, walked across the road to Number Six, with Mel.

"You were right," Mel said abruptly. "The place was in an awful state."

The social worker wouldn't understand, but suddenly Mel wanted her to see what she had done. Dee Tracey was expecting, Mel knew, to find the same confusion and dirt she had seen when Mrs Calder had been taken away, but Mel had worked like a galley slave spring-cleaning every evening after school.

Outside, waiting for the dustmen, was a pile of flattened boxes, tied up, with five plastic sacks of newspaper pieces. Everywhere was scrubbed clean, reeking of bleach. A lot of the smell had gone.

Dee Tracey's nose twitched.

"I can open the windows now," Mel said, mildly amused. "Mr Miller came over and showed me how to repair the window sashes." It was the first triumph. The first step on the long road and she had duly recorded it on the first page of her Project Diary, with a how-to-do-it diagram and a piece of sash cord.

Dee Tracey stared around at the old-fashioned furniture, now revealed in all its shabby ugliness. Taking up most of the space was the heavy oak table with bulbous legs and four dining chairs with tall backs, their seats split and peeling. Against the dividing wall was an enormous black mahogany sideboard with mirrors and tiny shelves and pillars holding them up. There were built-in cupboards either side of the boarded-up fireplace, and in front, a greasy carpet, its original colour impossible to see. The lino was worn to its backing by the door. Most of the surfaces were still covered with a jumble of papers, clothes, bags, boxes, frozen food containers. The wallpaper and ceiling were brown, discoloured with age, and little light came into the room through the single narrow window overlooking a chaotic back yard. But the floor and the table were clear now, and Dee Tracey saw that Mel had scrubbed the brown lino.

"Come and see upstairs." Mel led the way. She was proud of the amount of work she had accomplished in a few days and wanted Dee Tracey to see it all.

Her mother's room was clean now. She had nearly thrown up, cleaning it. She had stripped the bed of its grey, stinking sheets, and bundled them together into the dustbin. They were beyond washing. Under the bed had been piles of stained and smelling underwear covered with fluff and dust. She had taken these, with the curtains and blankets, round to the launderette. She had swept the walls free of cobwebs, scrubbed the paintwork and floor, cleaned the windows and rehung the curtains. But it still looked gloomy, the wallpaper dark, the furniture cheap and nasty.

Her own bedroom was always clean, but looking at it through Dee Tracey's eyes, Mel realised how poor it was. There was no carpet on the floor, and the faded pink cotton bed cover was torn. The only other furniture was a built-in cupboard and a small chest of drawers which she used as a desk to do her homework. A plaster cat Lucinda had given her for her fifteenth birthday sat on the windowsill, propping up her school dictionary and a few books.

"You want to look in the lavatory too?" Mel asked, sardonically. "It's downstairs outside, through the kitchen. It's got a rather interesting wooden platform, but we don't, of course, have the privilege of a bath."

"There's no need to be embarrassed, lovey."

"Isn't there?" said Mel.

They clattered down the narrow, uncarpeted stairs again.

Dee put her hand on the front room handle, but Mel shook her head. "We don't use it. It's empty. It's always locked. She thinks burglars are trying to get in through the front window."

They went along the short passage into the kitchen. An old cracked sink, an ancient water heater above. A grey marbled gas cooker. But everything was scoured. There were no unwashed plates or decaying food.

Dee said, without thinking, "How do you manage without a fridge?"

Mel clenched her hands until the nails cut into her palms.

"She was saving up."

"For a fridge?"

"For a fitted kitchen. They've all got them in this road, you know."

Dee Tracey said, "Mel, for heaven's sake. I'm not criticising. It's our job to try to help."

"Oh yeah? Funny nobody's bothered before. *Three years.*"

Dee flushed. "You have no idea how overworked we are, Mel. There are so many problems. Can't we try to be friends? At least we're trying to help now."

"You're too late," said Mel: "I realised I can do a better job for myself."

"Mel, are you sure you wouldn't rather stay with your aunt?"

"I told you, she's my *mother's* aunt, and I'm not going there. I'd much rather be with Mrs Miller. She's a great cook, and I can come in and do things to this place. I'm going to redecorate the living room as a surprise for my mother. It's going to be part of my art exams, and Mr Edwards is going to help me."

"Well that seems to be a very worthwhile idea, lovey." Dee sounded vague. Already her mind was on her next client, Mel thought. "I'll drop by next week to see if everything is okay. Your Social Security claim is sorted out?"

Mel nodded. "And the hospital have dealt with the rent of the house for my mother."

She had come to an arrangement with Mrs Miller about board and lodging, which left Mel with a larger amount of money in her pocket than she thought she ought to have. But Mrs Miller told her to buy some paint with the extra money. "I have my guilty feelings too, Mel," she had said. "I ought to have done something. We all knew what was going on."

"By the way," Dee Tracey said, turning back from the front door. "I forgot to say, I think you've done a marvellous job here. It looks a different place already. If you need me, call me. Don't forget. Any problems at all, call me."

"Yes, well . . . thanks."

Perhaps she had misjudged Dee Tracey. Maybe under all that posing professionalism she really did care. All the same, hell would freeze over before she called Dee Tracey for anything. *Lovey.*

Five

Mel had begun to spend all her spare time at Number Six, working obsessively. Every evening she would join the Millers for a meal, help wash-up, then walk across the street and let herself into her own cold, empty house, to work for another two or three hours. Sometimes it was hard to leave the cosy family warmth, with Ben and Stevie cheerful and jokey in front of the television, but she was driven by a determination that she could hardly explain even to herself.

Despite all the cleaning and getting rid of the boxes, the worst smell was still there. Using her nose, Mel tracked it down at last to the carpet in the living room, and then she could not stop thinking about it. Every time she came into the room she looked at the carpet. It was black with dirt, and grease had collected into hard, shiny spots like shellac. She tried to scrape them off with a knife and a scrubbing brush but it was a hopeless task.

She sat back on her heels and looked at the carpet for a long time, then, with sudden resolution, she jumped up, moved the table and chairs off it, rolled it up, tied it into the smallest possible bundle and dragged it outside the front door to wait for the refuse collection.

Saira Hussain came out of the house next door and watched her uneasily. She was three years younger than Mel, but sometimes they had walked to school together.

"But what will your mother say?"

"I don't *care!*" said Mel. "I don't care if she does tell me off. I'm not living with that stinking thing any longer. It's better without it. I'm trying to clean up. Come in. You might as well see what it's like."

Mel did not care any more. Let them all see. They might understand then what she'd had to put up with. She didn't think Saira would make jokes or be shocked.

Saira was silent, looking around.

Mel looked around too and began to laugh hysterically. "You know what? When the holidays start next week, I'm going to throw out all those nasty chipped ornaments on the shelf as well, I've always hated them. *And* this smelly old cushion. And that big broken clock . . . A-and that television. It can't be repaired. The man told her."

"She'll kill you."

"I'm going to throw out everything that can't be repaired or cleaned. I don't see why we've got to live in junk. It just makes you feel dirty and hopeless. That's the trouble with this house. This *road*, even. It's full of broken-down junk. There's nothing nice or beautiful to look at." She kicked the ugly table legs.

"There's a lot to do. I'll help you," said Saira.

Mel said stiffly, "I can manage. Thanks."

"But I'm good at cleaning up. We'll get it done more quickly."

It was funny, Mel thought bitterly, when she really needed help there was nothing. Now, when she was looking after herself, they were all pushing in.

Vi Brown, over the road, had said, "If you want a bed or a loan, come over. The Town Hall wouldn't like it, but don't let that stuck-up little madam in the red Volvo mess you about. I know how to sort out people like that. Tell her to eff off."

Mel had grinned. "Dee Tracey. She's not bad."

Mary Molloy in the end house said, wearily, "If you've

any laundry, Mel, I'll do it. Sure, there's so many of us, one more wouldn't make the difference."

And Mr Singh in the corner shop had insisted on giving her a bar of chocolate and a pack of pitta bread. "Come to us if you need food," he said. "You must not starve. We will always help."

All the street seemed to know her business, thought Mel, ungratefully, although *how* they knew was a mystery, as none of them ever spoke to each other. Except for the children, everybody detested everybody else, and kept themselves to themselves.

Mel stared at Saira angrily. Saira smiled at her tentatively. "You took me to school and helped me when I came and did not know anyone. I would like to help you now."

"Oh, all right," Mel said awkwardly. "You can help if you like. I'm going to sort out cupboards and things."

Once she had thrown out the carpet, Mel found it easy to throw away other things. She became ruthless in a wild orgy of clearing out, starting with the sideboard.

The top was covered with a jumble of paper bags, catalogues, old food packets, dirty clothes, old milk bottles, and frozen food foil trays with the remains of food adhering to them. It was all swept away into plastic sacks. The cupboards in the alcoves on either side of the fireplace were also piled high, and when these had been cleared, Mel turned her attention to the cupboards and drawers themselves. Her mother hadn't looked into the cupboards for years, so how could she possibly object to the rubbish being thrown out at last? Everything was cracked, chipped or torn. In all the cupboards and overflowing drawers there was not one thing worth keeping.

It wasn't even their own rubbish, Mel realised suddenly, dumping a box full of broken electrical bits and ancient two-pin plugs into yet another rubbish bag. All this must have belonged to the old man who had lived here before. The alcove cupboards were full of battered biscuit tins and small cardboard boxes crammed with screws of newspaper, each containing a few rusty nails, bits of clocks, nuts and bolts.

Mel stared at them, mystified. Why on earth had the old man kept them so carefully?

Rusty screws . . . boxes of newspaper squares . . . books . . . pop star pictures . . . it was all the same. Why did anybody collect anything? For *comfort*. He must have been screwy like her mother. Screws—*screwy* . . . Mel tried to laugh. The only comfort a few electrical bits or torn paper squares.

She threw the tins and their contents into the rubbish bag violently and found herself crying with rage.

Ever since her mother had been taken away, Mel had been permanently angry, filled with a vast impotent rage against somebody or something. Dee Tracey? Her mother? Fate? God? She didn't know, but she worked furiously, clearing the drawers and cupboards, tipping the rubbish directly into the plastic sacks. The worst of the war was inside herself, she realised. Hate, rage, guilt. She felt she wanted to kill someone.

"But oughtn't you to look through them?" said Saira, holding the bag for her. "There might be something valuable . . ."

"In *this*? It's junk, rubbish, *filth*, and we've lived with it all these years. But I swear I'm going to get rid of every last bit of it. It's been rising and rising and it's so high it's nearly choked us. Maybe it *has* choked my mother."

In the kitchen, the cupboard under the stairs was filled with rusty baking tins, broken saucepans and filthy pieces of old carpet, green with mildew. Dirty, sweating and swearing, she dragged them out one by one into the small back yard. It took another two days to scrub the cupboard clean with detergent and strong bleach. And then only the dresser was left: two cupboards, four drawers. Mel took more care here, not wanting to throw out any useful cooking things. But apart from the one cupboard which they used for their own small stock of saucepans and chipped china, and one cutlery drawer, Mel found, once again, the rest were full of the strange screws of paper packed into small boxes. Three matches in one. Two haricot beans in another, each wrapped carefully in three pieces of newspaper, dated 1963.

When the last drawer, cupboard and shelf were emptied and scrubbed, Mel felt a great wave of jubilation. It had taken nearly three weeks of constant work but it was worth it.

The whole place looked bare and strangely unlived in. Mel realised suddenly how little furniture there was. Just the square dining table with the dining chairs, and the huge, hideous sideboard standing on the worn lino.

She decided that the time had come to take the 'Before' photographs for her art project, and to start the decorating.

"You should have taken the pictures with all the boxes," said Saira.

"No. I didn't want people to see that," Mel said, embarrassed. "She couldn't help it."

"What about the front room? Are you going to paint that too?"

"I might," said Mel, "if I have time before she comes home. I don't know how long she'll be there. I'll take a couple of snaps of each room anyway. Just in case. We've never used the front room. It's empty."

Mel found the key on a nail in the kitchen and unlocked the door.

The room was packed to the ceiling with more cardboard cartons. There was the familiar, musty stench.

Mel felt physically sick. How *long* had her mother been mad? She wanted to sit down on the floor like a little child and howl with disappointment and rage. Just when she thought everything was clear, *this* . . .

Saira looked at her and looked away. She said, hurriedly, "There are not so many as it seems. We can soon clear them. Today, easily. Let's start now."

Mel closed her mouth grimly. She went into the kitchen and fetched some more plastic sacks, unable to trust her voice.

They worked in silence, emptying the newspaper squares, lugging the bundled boxes into the yard. Mel worked violently, slamming the boxes flat, tears of rage and anguish sliding unnoticed down her cheeks. After a while Saira stopped and made tea for them, and Mel began to feel better. Stupid, allowing a few boxes to upset her after all the unpleasant work. This time it really was the last. She had no intention of turning out the cupboards in her mother's bedroom. Perhaps when she came out they would do it together and redecorate the room too, but now she had enough to do downstairs.

They cleared the cartons in record time, leaving the room nearly empty, except for a small sofa with a tall back, split and stained with the stuffing coming out, a dusty grey carpet and three wooden packing cases full of carefully wrapped packages.

The boxes revealed treasures. A bone china tea set. Bed linen and towels. Curtains. Cushions. And folded into polythene bags at the bottom, two natural sheepskin rugs. A waste paper basket. A bamboo plant stand.

"These are our things," said Mel, pouncing delightedly. "I'd forgotten about them. We had them in the house in Scotland. She wouldn't unpack them here. But when everything is decorated, I'm going to put them out. I don't care what she says. I think it's stupid not to use them. What are we keeping them *for?*"

"Anyone about?" They heard Lucinda Miller calling. She lounged in through the open front door and stared around. "What have you done with everything?"

"In the yard," Mel said, ruefully. "The dustmen will only take a few bags at a time."

"What in God's name is *this*? I never noticed it before."

"A Victorian sideboard with overmantel, circa 1885," Mel said, grinning at Lucinda's expression. "Okay, I looked it up in a furniture book."

"What a horrible thing. All those little curly shelves sticking out like fungus. There was a thing like that in the monster film I saw last week. They blasted it with a laser and it just melted into a puddle of red blood."

They all three stared at the sideboard imagining it melting into the lino. And then Mel suddenly started to laugh. She went on laughing and could not stop. Her resentment and anger began to drain away. For the first time in years she felt the tension relax inside her. A small sprout of hope, alive and real, lifted itself from the darkness.

Six

The problem of the uncollected rubbish was becoming acute. Mel had put it all out for the dustmen, but they took two bags and left the rest, including the carpet. Disappointed, but not really surprised, Mel had dragged the stuff into the back yard which was already full of dismantled sheds, wooden boxes, and unidentifiable trash. There were even panels of corrugated metal which old Mrs Martin next door said were part of an air-raid shelter left over from the last war.

"What am I going to do?" Mel said despairingly to Mrs Martin. "I'm never going to get rid of it. I keep throwing stuff out and they don't take it. The back yard is full."

"Leave it to me," said Mrs Martin, grimly. "I'll see to them. Have you got an extra door key?"

When Mel came home from the market a few days later Mrs Martin was on the watch for her, sitting in her usual place by the front window, peering out between the net curtains in the space between the pot geranium and her ginger tom cat.

"Have a look in your yard," she said, laconically.

Mel raced through the house to the back door and flung it open. She stared disbelievingly. Everything had gone. *Everything.* The yard was as bare as the school showers.

They had left a trail of broken bits through the kitchen and ripped the wallpaper on the way to the front door, but the rubbish had all gone. For the first time she could see the wall at the end, the back of a factory in the next road, and the two tall wooden fences of the next yards. Under all the rubbish the weeds had tried to grow. Perhaps, if she dug up the rock-hard earth she might be able to grow some flowers . . .

"But they've taken it *all*," she told Mrs Martin, incredulous. "The bags. The carpet. The old shed. The rabbit hutches. *Everything.*"

"Well, you didn't want any of it did you? Rat harbourer, that's what that yard is. A nasty rat harbourer. I've seen them cleaning their whiskers on the coal box. I told him who lived there before you, but he never took no notice. We didn't get on, you know. Grumpy old sod. Queer in his attic, like your mum."

Mel said, trying to laugh, "Must be the house. I'll be next."

"Get away! Used to be a happy house when I was first married. Nice family. Two little girls who . . ."

Mel said, hastily, "But Mrs Martin, what did you *do*? They took it all. I couldn't even get them to take the dustbin bags."

Mrs Martin began to cackle. Mel watched fascinated. She had never seen Mrs Martin laugh; she was always in too much pain with her arthritis or too angry with the state of the world.

"We haf our messods . . ." Mrs Martin said, in a television Gestapo voice, and cackled some more. It took her a while to recover.

Mel said, intrigued, "Don't tell me you bribed them."

Mrs Martin closed one eye very slowly. "Blackmail. It's cheaper. It's my niece. Well, my niece's husband. He's the Environmental Health Officer for the Borough!"

Mel began to laugh too. So you could get things done if you knew the right person to talk to. What about all that stuff on the railway embankment, then? They could take all that too. She had a thing about the embankment rubbish since she had fallen into it. The street would look so much better if it

50

was all cleared. They could plant some flowering trees instead. And why couldn't they get the old dumped cars cleared and the roads swept too?

That evening, Mel talked it over with Lucinda as she got ready to go out.

"Are you crazy? Trees and daffodils—with the Molloy kids down the end here? You haven't a hope!"

"Well, at least we could get the rubbish cleared. It's just next to your house. You can't want it there."

"I don't care. I won't be living here much longer."

Lucinda was in her bedroom, rubbing cream into her skin. She looked after her skin very carefully. It was smooth and pure, a deep golden brown, like some exotic fruit, with a faint purplish bloom on it.

Mel perched on the end of her bed, watching. Lucinda was beautiful, she thought. Tall, cool, with a fantastic lithe body. Since she had left school she had grown even more beautiful. She was very sophisticated now. She knew just what clothes to choose and how to move in them.

She had resisted her mother's determination to make her stay into the Sixth Form, surviving the secondary plan to turn her into a nurse. She wanted something with big money in it, she insisted, to her mother's disgust. A *load* of money. She had it all planned. She was going to be a top model, then get into the video and film business. Already she had appeared on the cover of a new magazine for young Blacks called *Gold Rush*, and had modelled a sequined cloche hat for *The Face*.

Mel had been excited, but Lucinda had been casual about it. It was a beginning—just a beginning. She was not at all conceited about her looks, just coolly calculating about her assets, her feet very firmly on the floor. All the same, there was something unnerving and uncomfortable about her ruthless determination to get to the top. She seemed—Mel couldn't put her finger on it exactly—too cynical and hard,

51

as well as ambitious. That was what was cooling their friendship, not just the feeling Mel had that she was still a kid and Lucinda had somehow left her behind. She moved restlessly.

"So what's up?" said Lucinda, looking at Mel's reflection in the mirror.

"How did you know?"

"You let it all hang out, baby. As clear as crystal."

"I'm fed up. Our front door looked so grotty, I thought I'd have a go at painting it. A nice bright red. But all this street rubbish keeps blowing against the wet paint. They never seem to sweep down this road. How come the roads up near the Town Hall are all nice and swept and the streets down here are buried under loads of litter?"

Lucinda started to put on some gold eye make-up, to match the incredibly tight, shiny gold dress she was wearing. "Because up in those houses people write *letters* when they're upset. They make nasty *phone calls* to important people. Not like round here. The people here would lie down in the road and let someone drive a bus over them if somebody told them to."

Mel laughed. "Your mum?"

"Yeah. My mum too. The people here make me sick. They're so downtrodden. Never make an effort to do anything about anything. Take Mrs Molloy over the road. All those kids—nowhere to bath them. Outside lavatory. Why doesn't she go to the Council and kick up hell? Make them find her a better place. Kids ought not to be brought up like that."

"She's too tired," said Mel. "She hasn't got the energy. You might not if you had five kids under ten and a husband gone off somewhere."

"It'd make me worse," said Lucinda. "Mind you, I'd never get into that situation in the first place. Five kids? Hasn't she heard of birth control?"

52

"They're not allowed to. Catholics."

Lucinda shrugged contemptuously. "The Pope going to bring them up? And snotty Nicholls next door with his lawnmower, looking at you as if you're dirt. A lawnmower, I ask you! For a patch of dog shit, four by eight."

"Maybe he's too stiff to use clippers."

"And that Khan, keeping his wife shut up all the time. She never comes out at all."

"Maybe she's sick."

"I've not seen her once since she got here. How do we know he's not murdered her?"

"Oh come on, Lucinda! You don't really believe that."

"She may not be dead yet—but he's murdering her all the same. Murdering her mind. Keeping her shut up like that without friends. And why do they keep their curtains pulled all the time?"

Mel said impatiently. "They have to keep the curtains pulled in Pakistan because of the hot sun . . ."

"Hot sun. In *England*? That's good."

Mel could not help laughing.

"And there's Mrs Hickey, Nosey Flo, like a Russian border guard on the corner, so you can't blow your nose without she knows all about it. And Vi Brown. She's a slag. *Lovely* people."

"I like Vi Brown. She's all right," said Mel. "She offered to help. How do you know she's a slag?"

Lucinda snorted. "All those different cars? A new man every month?"

"So what?" said Mel. "It's nothing to do with us."

"Lewering the twone of the neebourhood," Lucinda said, in Mrs Nicholls's pinched accents.

"White trash?" suggested Mel.

"You said it, not me," Lucinda grinned. "And what about Mr Superior Singh in the shop?"

"He's really nice," said Mel, annoyed. "And so are the

53

Hussains next door to me. I like Saira. She's a friend. She helped me clean up the house."

"Think they're better than we are."

"Better educated, anyway," said Mel. "Mr Singh has a degree."

"Calcutta B.A.—failed."

"No it's not. It's a law degree. Honestly, Lucinda, you really cheese me off sometimes lately. You're becoming a racist, like Mr Nicholls."

"I don't like people looking down their noses at me."

"He doesn't. Mr Singh is studying for his English qualifications, and when he gets them he'll be able to be a solicitor."

"I'll believe it when it happens," said Lucinda, standing up and smoothing out her skirt. "You know something? None of this lot are ever going to get out of this street. Not *one*."

"Just you!" said Mel, furious, because Lucinda had finally put into words what she felt herself, but couldn't bear to face.

"Yeah, *me*, of course. And you too, maybe. Sometime. Everybody else will still be here. Even mum and dad. They've been saving for years to buy their own place. But they'll never move. Even Ben."

"How am *I* supposed to get out? Win the football pools? Join the army?"

"You'll get married," Lucinda said, deadpan, knowing how irritating Mel would find this.

"Billy Bell, in Sylvan Street?" Billy was a shambling lout in the next street, who spent his free time sitting on the edge of the pavement, his fingers in the zip of his jeans.

Lucinda looked her over coolly. "No, I think you can do a bit better. You'll never make the cover of *Gold Rush*, of course," her eyes gleamed provocatively, "but you're looking a lot better since we've been feeding you up. Nice eyes. Sexy bum and knockers."

Mel went red. "*Thanks very much!* Your mum ought to hear you."

" 'Go wash your mouth out with soap, chee-ild!' " agreed Lucinda, grinning. "But it's true. And it's what the boys notice."

"I've got other things to think about," Mel said, distantly.

"Yeah? Such as?"

"Decorating the house. A levels. Finding a Saturday job. My mother . . ."

". . . Keith Edwards."

Mel went red again. Lucinda looked at her shrewdly and sighed loudly. "So it's true! Well you certainly know how to make trouble for yourself, Mel."

"I don't know what you mean. He's my Group Tutor."

Lucinda laughed raucously. "Looking after you like a father."

Mel felt hot. "No! But . . ."

"Don't change the subject. You know what I mean. You fancy him. A lot."

Mel pretended to laugh. "You're crazy. He's my teacher. He'd never look at me."

"He'll do more than look if he gets the chance. Take it from your experienced Auntie Lucinda, keep out of his way."

Mel was surprised at her own fury. "He's not like that. He's *not*. You're talking through your hat. You don't even know him."

"I've seen him coming out of your place and I've seen the way he looks at me. I know the type."

Mel choked. "He's really good . . . Helpful . . . You're making everything dirty."

Lucinda shrugged. "Don't say I didn't warn you."

Seven

Mel worked all day and through the long summer evenings. The decorating was going well, but it was tiring and took longer than Mel had thought. She had painted the living room ceiling first. It seemed the obvious place to start, and white emulsion was the cheapest paint. Once-over, non-drip, the can said. It had taken *three* coats before the brown discoloration had been covered. True, it did not drip. Rather it dropped in big blobs or ran down her arms, which felt as though they were coming out of their sockets after a couple of hours holding them over her head. By the third coat she had learned the trick of taking smaller amounts of paint on the end of the brush, and moving the stepladder she had borrowed from Mr Miller into the right positions so the paint didn't drop on to her face.

Thankfully, she had now started on the woodwork, washing and rubbing down with sandpaper and wire wool as the decorating books she had got from the library advised. She was hoarding her money to pay for the white gloss paint and undercoat. White to cover all the dingy brown and make it light and cheerful.

If only she could find a Saturday job. She had inquired all around in the local shops without success. Nobody was taking on any Saturday girls. If she could find a Saturday job she could save up for the paint and all sorts of things. The Dream Desk, for instance.

She had seen it six months ago in a small junk shop in one

of the roads off the High Street. It was love at first sight. The desk was beautifully made in figured walnut, full of intriguing little drawers with brass handles and a carved rail round the top to hold books. Once it had been in the window with a card on it which said 'Snip £250' but now it was at the back of the shop. When she passed she always looked for it, always fearing it had been sold. If she had a desk like that, even homework would be a pleasure.

More realistically she could save up for an armchair. It would be really nice to have an armchair, Mel thought, wistfully. Somewhere soft and comfortable to sit and read a book. Surely she could get a very cheap armchair somewhere? She began to look at armchairs in furniture shops. They were huge and overstuffed and surprisingly expensive. One of these chairs would practically fill up the whole room in Cowcross Street, but she continued to look, hoping to find a broken one which she could repair. It was not until she had finished painting the woodwork white, and had begun to paint over the old wallpaper in the living room with a brilliant yellow emulsion paint, that she saw the ideal chair. It had appeared in the same junk shop as the desk.

She passed the shop often on her way to the market. It was a real junk shop, full of boxes of old lampshades and chipped vases, funny dressing tables, broken wardrobes, rusty fridges and cookers in the outside yard.

The chair was just inside the shop door. It was small, covered in dark green velvet, with a tall buttoned back, low arms and stumpy curved legs. Victorian, thought Mel, pleased that she was beginning to recognise some of the furniture styles illustrated in the interior decorating books she pored over avidly in the library.

Every time she passed she pushed her nose against the window to see it better, not daring to go in. What was the point? The chair was not broken. It would cost too much. But the shape was just right for the front room. She sighed.

57

On Friday evening she stood there for a long time. The old man who kept the shop was usually playing cards on a packing case with a crony in the yard beyond the side arch. If he had been there as usual she might have asked the price, but he was nowhere to be seen. Someone would buy the chair on Saturday and it would be gone forever. She noticed that there were delicate carved leaves spreading over the curved legs. It was crazy even *looking*. She had no money at all. She turned to go and then turned back and pushed open the door.

There was a young man sitting with his feet up on the desk that served as a counter, his chair tilted back.

"Congratulations! So you finally made it."

He put his paperback down and swung his legs to the floor. He had very dark blue eyes, almost black, which gleamed at her mockingly.

Mel stared at him, confused, her mind still on the chair. "Made what?"

"Made it inside. You've been hanging round here twice a day for a week, looking in the window."

Mel was embarrassed. "So what?"

"I don't bite. You could have come in."

"I'm just looking. That's what shops are for, aren't they?"

"Not shops like this. Who'd want any of this junk? You want my autograph?"

"*Autograph?*" She glanced at him, then looked again. His tee shirt was ragged and stained, his jeans shredded, and his dirty trainers had holes in the toes. His face, thin, bony, alive, looked clean enough, but his dark hair was unfashionably long and ragged, and didn't look as though it had been combed too recently.

She laughed. "How much is the small armchair?"

"Chair?"

"The one by the door."

"Aw, come on! You're not interested in furniture."

Mel said, annoyed, "Are you selling this stuff or not?"

"Getting married then?" His eyes laughed at her.

Mel said stiffly, "Plenty of girls get married at seventeen."

"Not you." His eyes flicked over her. "You're not pregnant. Too scared. Not interested."

Mel flushed. She said, sarcastically, "You know of course."

"Right." He grinned provocatively. "I know a lot about girls. I'm in a band."

She looked him over again, from the dirty trainers to the dishevelled hair, and began to laugh. "Sure," she said. "You and John Taylor."

Still laughing, she turned and walked out, pleased with herself, until she remembered she hadn't found out the price of the armchair.

On Monday the armchair was still in the shop, but the rude boy seemed to have gone. She could see the old man through the arch, in the yard, drinking a can of beer.

There was no harm in *asking*, after all. She hesitated, her heart quickening its beat. She went into the shop and prodded the buttoned back of the chair, leaving the shop bell jangling.

The old man came in reluctantly from the yard. "What do you want?"

Mel looked at him coldly. Some salesmen in this place! "How much is this armchair?"

He was small, stocky, wearing a thick navy jersey. He looked super-clean, his hair gleaming white, his skin red and creased, a humorous London face that had seen everything. He grinned at her derisively. "You're a bit young to be buying furniture, aren't you?"

Mel said angrily, "My money's as good as anyone's isn't it?"

59

"Sorry I spoke. Bit jumpy aren't we?"

"I know I look young, but I'm not a kid and I'm not shop lifting or after your till either."

"Did I say you were?"

"That's what you thought."

"You'll be glad you look young in a few years. How old am I?"

Seventy-four? She hated old people asking. "Sixty-eight," she said, to be polite and found herself grinning.

His eyes gleamed appreciatively. He looked like a bright-eyed monkey. "Yah, flattery! Eighty-five. I've lived about five times longer than you. Two World Wars and a bloody awful peace in between."

Mel was surprised. *Eighty-five.*

"Don't you want to retire?"

"Sit by the fire, nodding off? Dying by inches?"

"I just thought . . ."

"You see—you put me in a category too." His eyes were bright with triumph. "We all do it without thinking. Eighty-five equals old equals senile." He made a rude noise with his mouth. "Anyway, I *have* retired. The sea was my business. All the seas from the Baltic to the Pacific. First mate. You want to know what a Bangkok cat house is like, come to me."

"A *what?*" said Mel.

He grinned. ". . . when you're older." He waved his hand around contemptuously. "This dump keeps my bossy son off my back. Got to keep my business going, haven't I? I don't fancy a nice comfortable retirement home. Very cramping to my style. No betting shops in a home, sweetheart. No beer either, I shouldn't wonder."

Mel smiled at him. "You'd find a way round the rules."

There was an answering gleam in his eyes. "You're on my wavelength, sweetheart. Forty pounds."

60

"Forty pounds?"

"You asked about the chair."

"I can't afford it." Mel was disappointed, but not surprised. As well say a hundred and forty. She looked at the chair again, wistfully. It had been a good chair in its time. The green velvet was only slightly worn and she was sure that carpet cleaner and a nail brush would take off the stain on the arm.

"Genuine Victorian nursing chair. Very comfortable. A snip."

"I haven't got forty pounds."

"Try it."

Mel sat down. He was right. "It's lovely," she said, sighing. "Just right." She patted the low arms.

"Send your mum round. She may give you a birthday present."

Mel got up. She said in a hard voice, "They wouldn't let her out. She's in the loony bin."

He paused, rolling a cigarettte, and looked at her. "That's not the right way to put it."

"It's the truth."

"*Mental hospital*. She's sick. A lot of people get sick today. It's all the stress, strain and worry."

Mel shrugged, impatiently.

"You might yourself one day," he said severely. "One woman in eight. There but for the grace of God go all of us, and don't you forget it."

Mel swallowed, suddenly paper-white.

He softened. "Depression? Schizophrenia?"

"Acute depression, they said."

His eyes were shrewd, understanding. "It's all right, don't worry. It's not hereditary. You don't have to end up there yourself."

Mel took a deep, shaky breath of relief. How had he known? "At school, the kids said . . ."

"Ignorant buggers. Take no notice."

Mel grinned painfully. "I'm trying to fix up the house. Redecorate. But it's not easy."

"What about your dad?"

"Dead. I want to make the house comfortable for my mother when she comes home. Then maybe she won't get ill any more."

"That's why you want the chair?"

"We haven't got any armchairs. Only kitchen chairs. And a table and one of those horrible great sideboards with mirrors and little shelves and curly bits. There isn't room for anything else. It takes up all the space." She was bitter. "Nothing comfortable or useful."

He looked thoughtful. "Well now . . . Maybe we can do business. I've had a dealer sniffing around for one of them sideboards. Getting fashionable up West."

"Fashionable?" Mel could not believe it. "Even if you had a big house—"

"They cut the tops off for the bathroom. Fit the cupboard in the kitchens. All good solid mahogany," he said, reprovingly.

Mel pretended to shudder, but all the time she was wondering if she *dared*. Her heart was banging against her ribs. Her mother would surely kill her. First the carpet, then the television, now she was getting rid of the furniture! But the room would look so much better without that dusty horror . . . there would be so much more space . . . and she would have a comfortable armchair to sit in . . .

"All right," she heard herself saying. "I'll swop, if you think the sideboard is worth forty pounds."

"I'll send someone round to look at it." He got out a stub of pencil and a grubby envelope. "What's your address, sweetheart?"

"Six Cowcross Street. My name's Mel."

"Nell. *Nelly Dean!* Well, if that isn't an omen." He folded back a copy of the newspaper and showed her. "See here, two-thirty at Worcester. *Nelly Dean.*"

"I'm Mel, not Nell," she protested, but he wasn't listening.

"I'll make it a double with *Sitting Pretty* in the three forty-five at Windsor. Want a flutter? Go on. It can't lose. Thirty-three to one. I'll put it on for you."

"How much?" said Mel, cautiously, looking in her purse. "I've only got twenty pence."

"That'll do. We'll go the whole way. No pansy place betting. Do it to win. It's a dead cert."

"Are you sure?"

"Certain as this is Tuesday."

"It's *Monday!*" Mel laughed. "Oh, all right. Let's live dangerously."

They didn't win. Both horses came second.

A few evenings later there was a knock at the front door. Mel climbed down reluctantly from the stepladder—she was spreading a second coat of the sunny yellow emulsion paint over the old wallpaper—and found the young man from the junk shop on the doorstep.

She hardly recognised him. He was wearing brand-new jeans, an expensive-looking leather jacket and his hair had been cut and brushed by a master hairdresser. She, on the other hand, was wearing her working outfit—her oldest jeans, and a tee shirt which had fitted when she was twelve, but which now failed to make contact with her jeans by a good six centimetres. Both of them were daubed with the various paints she had used so far. She had pinned up her hair to keep it out of the paint and there was a smudge of yellow on the tip of her nose.

He looked her over, his eyes full of laughter. She realised he was really very good-looking. But she did not like boys who looked at you like you were a Big Mac and they were working out which end to eat first. Irritably she tugged her tee shirt down and said, "What do *you* want?"

"Come to look at a chiffonier."

"A what?"

"Sideboard. Black mahogany."

"Oh. Oh yes. Come in." Somehow she had thought the old man would come himself.

She stood back for him to pass and tried to keep the excitement out of her voice. "It's in here."

"Christ!" said the boy. "He bought that? He's going soft-headed."

Mel glared at him. "He said he had somebody looking for one."

"Oh well, let's have a look. See if there's woodworm."

He pulled out a couple of drawers and looked at their backs.

"Is it all right?" asked Mel, hovering. "I mean, will you swop the chair for it?"

The boy glanced around the room. It looked even worse now, the furniture in the centre draped with polythene bags, the old lino covered with paint drips, the walls half-painted. It was chilly too, with a one-bar electric fire.

He smiled at her. "Okay, don't worry. I've got the chair outside in the van, but I can't manage that monster myself. I'll have to come back."

"I'll help," Mel said, eagerly. "The top comes off."

He laughed. "It's too heavy. You'll do yourself an injury. I'll fetch Lou."

"The old man who keeps the shop?" Mel was doubtful. "But, I mean, he's old, perhaps . . ."

"Don't let Grandad hear you. Strong as an ox. Fitter than I am."

"He's your grandad? I've never seen you in the shop before."

"Maybe you weren't looking. I'm generally there between

jobs. But I've seen you. You go to William Watt. Last year you used to walk home with a Black girl. A real looker."

"Yeah," Mel sighed. "Everybody notices Lucinda. She's left school now."

"I noticed *you*. You were having a bad time."

Mel stared at him blankly, remembering the night she had tried to tip herself in front of the train. Her face suddenly went white, her eyes huge. She shivered. "You could say that."

He put a finger under her chin and looked at her. His gaze made her feel uncomfortable and she shook him off, angry. She did not want anybody's pity.

He shrugged. "All right. Where do you want this armchair?"

He went out to the van and carried it in. Mel watched disbelievingly. She had actually acquired an armchair.

"I'll be back. Tomorrow, maybe."

"Fine," she said, absently, stroking the chair. It was exactly the right size for the room.

"Goodnight, Nelly."

"Mel."

"Oh my, *Milly!*" he said, in a ludicrous, mincing accent, sticking out his little finger. "Goodnight Millicent."

"M.E.L." said Mel, annoyed.

"Mel? What sort of a name is that? That's a boy's name. Oh, I know. Melanie. Like the wet lady in *Gone with the Wind*."

"No, it's not! If you must know, it's Melody. You think I'm going to call myself Melody?"

"Hey," he was delighted. "Melody. I really like that. Very appropriate. A good omen."

"What are you talking about?" she said crossly. "There's no need to be joking about it. It's an old Somerset name after my Gran. Anyway, I can't help it, can I? So what's *your* name—John Smith?"

"Michael Hamilton."

"Well, goodnight then, Mickey—remember me to Minnie!"

He laughed. "I haven't got a Minnie. My friends call me Mitch."

He seemed to be waiting—expecting some kind of reaction—or was it her imagination?

Mel said, carefully, "Goodnight, Mr Michael Hamilton." She shut the door and went back to gloat over the chair.

It was later when she was getting into bed that she thought about his name again. It was odd, but she felt she had heard that name mentioned at school recently. Mitch Hamilton. Maybe Ben Miller would know. He knew everybody.

They collected the sideboard the following evening.

"That's my grandson," said Lou proudly, as Mitch went back to the van for straps. He began to dismantle the top. "Nice lad. Brainy. Talented. Helps me out."

"Yes, we've met," Mel said, absently. "You *sure* somebody wants this thing?"

The room would look empty when it was gone. She wondered if the wooden connecting doors behind it could be opened to make one big through room.

Lou looked at her slyly and grinned, nudging her with his elbow. "Nice looking fella, eh? Good shoulders. Other parts all in working order. Could do worse."

Mel went red as Mitch came in, knowing he must have heard. His ears were rather pink but he was grinning. "You're a dirty old man, Lou."

"Romantic," said Lou, hefting one end of the huge sideboard base without apparent effort. "To you, my son. *Roman-tic*. All sailors are romantic."

In the following weeks of holiday and of the new school term, whenever she passed the junk shop Lou would wave to her.

Sometimes he gestured for her to have a cup of tea. If she had time she would stop and pick her way through the yard to where he was sitting with his old mate Syd who kept the betting shop along the road. She discovered they liked sweet things, and sometimes bought cream cakes for them from the baker's. Mitch Hamilton was nowhere to be seen.

"How's your grandson?" she said, at last. "I haven't seen him around for a while."

Lou put his head on one side like a bright monkey and grinned at her. "Missing him?"

"No," Mel said indifferently. "I just wondered if he'd found a job yet."

Lou said, "I've got a hot tip here. *Singing Star.* How'd you like to make a bit of money? Fifty-to-one. We'll play it safe. First three. Win or place."

"I lost twenty pence last time," Mel said, resigned. "It had better win this time. I really need some cash."

Singing Star came fourth.

She went in after school to complain to Lou about it and found Mitch Hamilton sitting with his feet up on the desk.

"Hello. What a shame—have you lost your job again?" Mel said, sympathetically.

"I've got a job. I'm just resting."

"Oh yeah?" Mel ran her eye over him satirically, looking pointedly at his dirty tee shirt and old jeans. "Go on, surprise me. You're a TV actor."

He grinned. "In show business anyway. I play in a band with my friend Barney."

Mel picked up her school bag. "I might have known it! Another music freak. You know, there are four boys in my tutor group who want to learn to play the guitar?"

"I didn't say I was learning. I said I played." He was annoyed.

Mel smiled nastily. "Sorry I spoke, Mr Clapton." She went off to do her homework, amused, forgetting all about him.

Eight

"It's easy," said Mr Miller, and demonstrated how to wield the electric sanding machine he was lending to her. "Just keep it moving, girl, or you'll have a hole in your floorboards."

His laughter rumbled in his chest, but Mel felt apprehensive. She had ripped up the holed lino in the living room and was going to attempt to sand and varnish the floorboards. The picture she had seen in *Ideal Home* had shown a golden satiny floor, absolutely smooth and gleaming, and it had seemed a perfect answer to her lack of money to buy carpets or vinyl for the living room.

As soon as she started she realised it had been a mad idea. Why did books and magazines always make it sound so *easy*? The sander was difficult to hold. It was too heavy for her hands and arms. They ought to make smaller tools for women, she thought irritably, trying to control the sander as it bucked and skidded over the uneven floorboards. The wood dust rose in suffocating clouds, covering her clothes, her hair, her skin.

Grimly she tied a scarf around her nose and mouth and another over her hair and went back to work. It took hours. The dust rose and clung to the newly painted walls. Despite the scarf she seemed to have swallowed pounds of the stuff. Her back felt as if it would break in two. Her shoulder muscles were in agony, but she worked on doggedly, inch by inch across the floor, determined not to give up. The floor seemed to stretch twice as big as it was before.

It took nearly three evenings, but at last it was done. She brushed the walls down carefully, relieved to see they seemed none the worse, and swept up yet another pile of wood dust. It still did not look like the *Ideal Home* picture, but two coats of polyurethane varnish improved it considerably, making it look as though the sun was shining into the room all the time.

"How did people get carpets clean before vacuum cleaners, Mrs Martin?"

"They beat them over the clothesline with a stick. Both sides—to get all the dust out. And then they scrubbed them!"

Mel groaned. She had decided to clean up the carpet in the front room, which was thick with generations of dust, but she had no cleaner and the stiff brush wasn't moving the dust at all. It looked like a very big job, but Saira said she would help, and a few days later they struggled out to the yard with it.

It was terribly heavy and full of dust and by the time they got it over the small line they were already hot and sticky. The carpet hung over the line only a few inches from the ground on either side, and the line post began to creak ominously.

They attacked the carpet from both sides with broom handles. Dust rose in suffocating clouds.

"It's thicker than I thought," said Mel, gasping.

"Yes, and look, it isn't grey after all. It's green with pink roses."

"It still needs cleaning."

"You can hire a machine to clean carpets. In Swingers. I don't think it would cost much for one day."

"Hey, that's a good idea! I didn't fancy having to scrub it. I think I'll keep it rolled up for now and put it down later. I

70

want to paint the front room too, now I've got the doors open. I was going to paint it yellow, like the living room, but now I'll have to think again. A very pale green maybe? I'll start this weekend."

"It looks much nicer now." Saira giggled. "Do you remember all those boxes?"

Mel said, "You know, Saira, you've helped me a lot. Not just the work you've done, but cheering me up too. That's even more important."

Saira said, shyly, "I like to help a friend." She paused. "Are you visiting your mother on Sunday?"

Mel nodded morosely. "As usual."

She hated the regular visits. There was the long Green Bus journey which seemed to take hours, then the long walk up to the hospital from the front gates. Always it seemed to be chilly and raining. And then the grey depression of the building took over. Not that it wasn't bright and well-painted inside, but there hung about it a miasma of depression and fear that the bright flowers could not dispel.

In her mother's ward they all seemed to sit about unspeaking. Her mother huddled in a chair, staring. Mel was never sure if she recognised her.

"The hospital say she's improving. I suppose they know. She doesn't look any different to me. I don't know what to say to her."

The ominous creaking which they had been conscious of grew worse, and they looked up, just in time to see the rickety line post sway and collapse heavily on top of the carpet. A last great billow of dust rose into the air.

"There you are! It's done it for us," said Saira, delighted.

On Sunday, after the visit, Mel went home gloomy and dispirited, to finish emulsioning the front room.

It was a disaster area.

Yesterday, as she painted the old wallpaper, bulges had

appeared. A similar thing had happened to the back room and it had dried perfectly flat again, but here the paper had not only remained bulgy, but was also hanging half-off the walls. It looked as though the old paste had dissolved. She saw at once that she would never be able to stick it back. It would all have to come off. Every bit of it.

She glared at it, and then began to rip it off viciously. Why was everything always so difficult? Why was it when you already felt down, something else hit you? All right, she thought, trying not to cry, I'll have to re-paper the walls. You don't know how, her mind sneered.

"Well, I'll just have to learn, won't I?" she shouted, aloud.

Nine

"We could try to do something," argued Mel to Lucinda, one evening. They were on good terms again. Mel had dismissed Lucinda's warning about Keith Edwards as sour grapes. It was just too silly. Keith was a good person. He was giving her a lot of help in the new term with her art project—showing her how to mount photos and colour samples properly, how to draw ground plans and sketches of proposed alterations, even how to do simple lettering for the labelling and headings, which made the folder look very professional. He was always asking her how things were, and he had a special smile, just for her, which made her heart flip over.

Mel went on, "We could *try* to get the street cleaned up. Everybody pays rates. It's not fair."

"Too many of us Blacks here," said Lucinda. "The Town Hall don't reckon there's any point in sweeping these streets—we'll only make 'em dirty again." She cackled at her joke, sounding very like Mrs Martin.

Mel did not think it was funny. She said, "Maybe Mrs Martin's nephew can do something."

But Mrs Martin said the refuse collection was different from street sweepers and she didn't think her nephew would be any good.

"All the same, I'll complain," she said. "Give me over that pad. I'll write a letter and you can post it."

Nothing came of Mrs Martin's letter. Several weeks went past.

Mitch Hamilton dropped in late one afternoon. He said he had come to see how the decorating was going on, and to give her a hand but he spent the time, to Mel's increasing annoyance, lounging in the polythene-draped armchair, one leg over the arm, watching her painting the ceiling of the front room. Watching *her*, rather than the painting, she discovered, looking round. She came hastily down the stepladder, wiping the paint from her arms.

"Haven't you got anything else to do?"

"No."

"There must be something more exciting."

"Are you offering?"

Mel coloured. She was no good at this kind of chat. He got up, laughing, and put his arm round her shoulders. "Come on, I'll make you a cup of tea."

She shook his arm off, embarrassed, and washed her brush under the tap, while he leaned against the draining board waiting for the kettle to boil.

"This dresser. It's nice. You ought to strip the paint off. It's pine."

Mel looked at it disbelievingly. "I don't believe it."

"Pine with brass handles. Look." He scratched one of the handles with his thumb nail and Mel saw the gleam of metal. "It would look good."

She stared at the dresser doubtfully. "It's a big job. All those fiddly bits. It'd take forever. It would be easier to paint it white."

"I'll tell you what," he said; hitching himself on to the kitchen table. "I'll come over and do it for you."

She looked at him suspiciously. "But why should . . . *How much?* I can't pay you."

He grinned. "For love."

She sighed, exasperated. "I would have thought you had enough to do in your grandad's shop. Aren't you looking for a job?"

"I've got a job. I told you—I'm resting. I'm a musician."

"Honestly?" Mel was only half convinced. She did not like the way he was grinning. "Well, don't you have to practise then?"

"Rehearse. Yes. But I've got time to do the dresser. I like that kind of thing."

"Thanks, Mitch, but I don't think . . ."

But he came anyway and spent three days scraping off the layers of paint while she was at school. He worked meticulously, attending to every detail, concentrated. Mel, who worked in a similar way, found it extremely irritating. She did not like to tell him that the dresser seemed to be looking worse, not better.

"When I've finished this, I'll make a matching built-in unit for the sink and draining board," he said. "We could do with more cupboards in the kitchen."

She stared at him. What did he mean 'We'? "You're joking."

He smiled, unaware of his lapse. "I'm not just a pretty face you know. Top of the woodwork class at Thomas Conway!"

"But your hands," Mel said, worried. "Ought you to be using tools? Suppose you have an accident? I thought musicians . . ."

He laughed. "Have a look."

He stretched out his hands so that she took them automatically. They were very strong, big. The fingers were scarred and there was hard skin on the inside of them.

"Three weeks on the road and they're raw. I'm not a concert pianist."

"Oh." She began to move her hands away, but his long fingers closed round hers, trapping them.

75

She looked up at him indignantly, and found he was looking back at her, unsmiling and intent, his eyes brilliant. Her heart began to beat irregularly for no reason she could think of.

Behind her, Lucinda said, "Well, hello lovebirds! Holding hands? How sweet!"

Mel snatched her hands away from Mitch, her face scarlet.

Lucinda raised an eyebrow. "If he's proposing I'll go out again."

Mel snapped, "Don't be stupid!" and went back to her painting, leaving Lucinda and Mitch grinning like idiots.

"My God, you have gone to town," said Lucinda, after Mitch had taken himself off. "I thought you were going to clean up and paint a bit. It looks like you've had the demolition men in, just after the burglars moved out."

Mel had scraped all the wallpaper off the walls of the front room, and was carefully repairing the plaster underneath. She looked around vaguely. Everybody who had been in recently had been shocked and surprised. No carpet or lino on the floor. The few odd pieces of furniture covered with black polythene rubbish bags. No curtains at the window. The strange mouldy smell of damp plaster everywhere. She grinned, suddenly, remembering how it had looked a few months ago, full of dirt and boxes. "You won't know it when I've finished with it."

Lucinda laughed. "I don't know it now. Suppose your mum comes home suddenly?"

Mel looked uneasy. "I can start the re-papering soon. It won't take me long now. Perhaps I have gone a bit over the top. It's the preparation that takes the time, and I have to put special stuff under the windows to stop the damp. Then I paint the woodwork and put the carpet down again."

Lucinda said, bored. "You got the wallpaper?"

"That thick stuff that looks like porridge. The man in the

76

shop said it would cover up all the bad walls. Then I'm going to paint it with pale apple-green emulsion paint. I think it will tone with the yellow in the back, and now that the dividing doors are open . . ."

Lucinda snorted with laughter. "*Removed* you mean!"

Mr Miller had been over, unscrewed the hinges and taken the doors away for Mel. "Suppose your mum wants to close them?"

"Why should she? It looks so much better with them gone. One big room is better than two tiny ones. More space."

Lucinda shrugged. "I'd like to see her face when she sees all this." She mimicked, "And Melody, *what* have you done with my Beautiful Sideboard? And my Beautiful Carpet and my Beautiful Television . . ."

Mel looked uneasy again. "But she's got an armchair now. And the pine boards look nice. Better than that filthy old carpet. When everything is done there's a sheepskin rug for the front of the fire . . ."

Lucinda laughed. "I was only joking. Look, you don't have to convince me. It's too late to be worrying now, Mel. Have they said anything about her coming out?"

"No, but she looked better when I went in last week. She looked quite plump. She knew who I was. And guess what? She was wearing jeans and a shirt!"

Mitch appeared again a week later, looking pleased with himself.

"You owe me a fiver!"

Five pounds? Mel's heart sank. He must know she couldn't afford five pounds for anything.

"What have you got?"

"Come and see."

She followed him out to Lou's van. "How's *that*, then? It came in this morning. I knew it would be just right for the living room."

Mel peered round his shoulder. At the back of the van there was a round pine table, nearly new, with four matching chairs.

"*Five pounds?* You can't mean it. It must have cost more than that."

"The woman wanted it taken away. She's gone in for High Tech. Grey tubular metal like a battleship."

"It's just fantastic! I can't believe it. But how am I going to pay you? I haven't got . . ."

He grinned. "In instalments. Twenty pence a week. Come on then, don't stand there like a statue. Let's get it in."

They carried the table and chairs into the house, and with more difficulty, carried out the old table and the high backed chairs with the cross bars underneath.

Mel began to laugh, nearly dropping her chair. *And Melody, what have you done with my Beautiful Solid Oak Dining Room Suite . . . ?*

The pine table on the pine boards by the window of the living room looked like one of the pictures she had seen in *Ideal Home*. She could put the new pottery bowl she had made at school in the centre, full of fruit and it would look . . .

"Well," said Mitch, behind her.

She turned to him, her eyes glowing. "Oh Mitch, it's fantastic. Brilliant. *You're* brilliant."

He stood grinning at her. "What about a thank you kiss then?"

"No!"

He put his arms around her. "Aw, come on, love. Don't I deserve it?"

It was true, he did deserve it. He had called in several times, helping to scrape and rub down the woodwork. Helping to put up shelves.

Before she could think about it and get even more embarrassed, she gave him a quick peck on the cheek.

"Call that a kiss?"

His arms tightened and he cuddled her against him, lifting her chin. His lips brushed hers, gently, slowly. They were warm, slightly moist. She hadn't thought a boy's mouth would feel like that. Something strange seemed to be happening to the muscles at the base of her stomach. She knew Mitch could feel it too, because he slid his hands into her hair to support her head and began to kiss her properly. The kissing seemed to go on a long time, getting deeper and wilder, until they were both shaking.

Frightened of her physical reaction, she pulled herself free and stood away from him, blushing furiously and trying to breathe normally, trying not to let him see how worked-up she was. She had no idea kissing did that to you.

What did you say after someone kissed you like that? Something cool. Something jokey. *Anything!*

"Well," he said, watching her. "How did you like it?"

"N-not bad," she said, still finding trouble with her breathing. "You're not the first boy to kiss me, you know."

He grinned delightedly. "You're shaking like a leaf. Hey, you're really turned on."

"So are you," Mel snapped, exasperated. "And if you don't go lock the van somebody'll nick it."

Mitch finished the dresser and Mel helped to rub linseed oil into the surface. The wood came up rich and satiny gold, the handles gleaming.

"Okay," said Mel, "I take it all back. It looks fabulous."

"You need some nice plates to put on it," he said, looking at it with satisfaction.

"I've got them," Mel laughed, excitedly. "The china we had in Lothian. It was in one of the packing cases, still wrapped up. I think I'll re-paper the kitchen. It's easy now I've got the hang of it."

"And I'll get on with the sink cupboard."

To her surprise he built it quickly and efficiently in less

than a week, and went away, saying he had some work and would not be around for a while.

Mel felt relieved. Lately he had been there nearly every evening, and since he had kissed her and looked at her in such a strange way, she had felt uncomfortable. It was not that she didn't appreciate his help—the sink cupboard was really great—but Lucinda kept asking how she was making out with her dishy boyfriend, and she felt increasingly embarrassed. He was nice, but she didn't want a boyfriend. At least . . . Keith Edwards' face flashed into her mind.

Well, Keith was something else. Perhaps when she left school next year, he would come round to see her and holding her hand he would smile into her eyes. "I've been waiting such a long time, Mel, my darling . . ."

She was annoyed to discover that she had been sitting daydreaming for nearly half an hour, and the kitchen ceiling had still not been completed.

The next day, Mel said casually to Ben Miller, "You heard of a musician called Mitch Hamilton?"

Ben looked at her for a moment and did his favourite demented Lenny Henry impression.

"Do I know Mitch Hamilton? Do I know the Mighty Diamonds? Do I know . . ."

"Well, do you?"

"Where you been, man?"

He pulled a folded, grubby fanzine from his back pocket and shoved it into her hands. It was for a group called Assassination. She stared at it astonished. The photograph was smudgy, the printing poor, but there could be hardly any doubt. It was Mitch, looking clean and glamorous, hair brushed into fashionable dishevelment, smiling sexily into the camera.

"Lead Guitarist," it said, *Mitch Hamilton*. She read the fanzine carefully. Mitch's biography seemed to be rather vague. Born in Surrey. School at Thomas Conway Comprehensive, the other side of the borough. Assassination had started there and gone from strength to strength.

"You must have heard of them," said Ben. "They're local. Everybody at school knows them. Their new single went up to Number Three last week, from Twenty-Seven. That's the second time they've had a big hit. You must have heard *Altered State*. Kind of rock-funk fusion." He jigged around the room, singing.

"Oh *that*," said Mel, impressed, recognising it. They were playing it all the time on Capital Radio.

It couldn't be the same person, Mel thought. What would a pop star be doing with his feet up in his grandad's junk shop in grotty old clothes, needing a shave and spending all his spare time scraping paint off an old dresser?

Resting, he had said. He played guitar, he said. He was in a band. It all tied up. And it explained the casual kissing. Everybody knew that rock musicians were into loose sex.

But where were the limos, the managers, the PR men, the photographers, the fans . . . ?

Suppose, though, he just wanted to get away from it all for a few hours? If he wanted some peace and quiet occasionally, it might be the perfect disguise.

She decided to say nothing, not even to Lucinda or Ben. It was too incredible, and if he was *the* Mitch Hamilton he was obviously keeping quiet about it. She was glad she had found out in time. No more kissing. One thing she was not about to do was go overboard for a rock star who'd be on his way to other girls in other towns and other countries before you could say "Can I have your autograph?".

Ten

To everybody's amazement, the Council had sent workmen round to inspect the gutters of the roofs in Cowcross Street. Mel, letting the men through the kitchen, found that the heavy overnight downpour had totally ruined the new wallpaper, put up so carefully and lovingly two nights before. The rain had seeped into the cracks of the glass roof. Dark yellow stains had spread down the flowery white wallpaper which had looked so good with the dresser. She swallowed.

"I don't know why you're bothering about the gutters," she said angrily. "What about the roofs? Can't you do something about all this water coming in the extension?"

He looked at the water dripping into a saucepan and up at the broken panes.

"How long's it been like this?"

"Years. Ever since we came."

The foreman was disgusted. "Your mother ought to have put in about it. Letting it get in this state."

"They don't do repairs round here!"

"They do if you ask the right people," he said. "You tell your ma to write in."

"She can't. She . . . she's . . ." Mel hesitated, and knew she must overcome her reluctance to say it. There was nothing disgraceful about being in a mental hospital.

"She's sick. She's in Hob's Green."

"Oh." He looked at her speculatively. He knew about Hob's Green. "Trying to manage on your own then?"

82

"Yes."

"That's brave. All right. William! Get down here. Look at this extension. Can you do anything with it? Patch it up?"

"Sure," said William. "Some new glass, bit of putty, new frame there. Good as new."

"I can't understand about all you people in a street like this," said the foreman to Mel, severely. "You can get things done you know, if you get together. You could get bathrooms and kitchens. Built-on extensions. They're doing it in other parts of the borough."

"Bathrooms!" For years Mel had longed for a bathroom, the way other people longed for a car or a holiday in the Bahamas.

"But are you sure? I mean, we haven't got any money. We can't pay."

"The Council pays. It's their property. They get money from the Government to clean up the slums. To bring things up to modern standards, see? You get yourselves called a General Development Area and they come and modernise the place. And there's grants for people who own their own houses."

"You'd never get the people round here together," said Mel, hopelessly. "They hate each other. They don't even say good morning."

The foreman stood looking morosely along the backs of the houses. "It's disgusting. People shouldn't have to live in places like this in this day and age. Should have been pulled down years ago."

"They could be made nice," said Mel, surprising herself. "I saw a little row of houses like this in Chelsea once, and they looked quite different. All neat and painted, like doll's houses. With window boxes."

"Oh yes, they could be converted. They're not badly built. Quite solid. Okay, William, get to it. If they want to know at the depot—the ladder slipped. Understand?"

83

William grinned. "Sure. My big boot went right through. Very narrow escape. I'll get down to the depot for the stuff now. Get it done this afternoon in case there's any more rain tonight."

"Oh thanks a lot!" Mel could hardly believe it. "If only you knew what a relief it'll be not having to catch the drips."

No letter had come about the road sweeping. The rubbish continued to pile up in the gutters.

"A campaign," said Mel. "That's what we need. A petition like at school about a tuckshop. We could get everyone to sign it and take it to the Town Hall."

"Great," said Lucinda. "There are ten houses in this road. They're going to take a lot of notice of twenty signatures."

"Not just Cowcross," said Mel, impatiently. "We can do Sylvan Street and Blossom Bank Road. And Market Street too. There are more houses in those roads."

Lucinda made a rude noise.

"Oh come on, Lucinda. You're always complaining how feeble everyone is. Why don't *you* do something?"

Lucinda groaned. "Oh well, all right. It's a waste of time, but I'll help."

They began by putting leaflets through every door in the four roads.

LET'S GET RID OF THE RUBBISH
Join our Campaign!

Mel had made a drawing showing dirty litter piled against an abandoned car for the leaflet, and Ben Miller had run them off illegally on the school photocopier, one evening after school, while Mel kept a shivering watch outside the office door.

They made house-to-house calls to collect signatures for the petition, and were surprised at the enthusiastic support. Everyone signed. Some people wanted to sign twice. *Everybody*, it appeared, felt sore about the litter in the streets.

The petition, with two hundred and eight genuine signatures and five suspect ones—Benjie the Budgie?—was received graciously into the Town Hall.

A week later they received an acknowledgement card but no reply letter arrived.

A letter to their elected Councillor brought a reply saying that the matter would be looked into.

They wrote to the Mayor, who invited them to join his Walk in aid of the Mayor's Fund; they wrote to the Chairman of the Environment and Amenities Committee, who referred them to the Race Relations Officer, and they wrote to the Chairman of the Cleansing and Engineering Committee, who wrote back saying that he personally had looked into the matter and it appeared that their streets had been swept adequately and regularly and he could only suppose that certain unreliable elements in the community were trying to stir up trouble. He had asked the police to investigate.

All these letters were taped to Mr Singh's corner shop window, so that everyone could follow the progress of the campaign. The letters aroused great resentment and indignation. From mild irritation, they converted the residents to angry militancy. Neighbours who had not spoken to each other before wagged their heads together, outraged and angry at each succeeding letter.

The rubbish continued to blow along the gutters.

"Try the Neighbourhood Advice Centre," suggested old Mrs Martin. "They have them free lawyers and such like there."

The lady in the Centre listened to their problem with tired sympathy. "Well, of course, street cleaning is always a problem, and to be fair the Council has been badly hit by the government cuts. They have to save money for more important things."

"They must be saving a lot of money on brooms," said Lucinda. "They won't wear out if the men go on dragging them along upside down."

"Well, don't give up." The woman smiled at them brightly. "Here's a list of people you could contact. They'll look into the matter for you."

Outside, they stared eagerly at the list.

> Write letters to:
> *Your elected Council representative.*
> *Chairman of the Environment and Amenities Committee.*
> *Chairman of the Cleansing and Engineering Committee.*
> *The Mayor . . .*

Mel went to see Lou, sitting on his packing case in the shed.

"It's no good. You can't get anyone to do anything. They keep passing you on to someone else. We collected all these signatures and they still haven't cleaned up. They say they'll look into it and then, *nothing*. You can't get anything done. It's a waste of time trying."

Lou looked at her. "Gonna let 'em walk all over you then?"

"Lou, it's no *good!*" Mel was annoyed. "We've tried. We really have. There's a kind of glass pane there. You can't get through it."

Lou rubbed his whiskers. "Joe Isaacs. That's who you want. A friend of mine. He'll get the rubbish removed."

"How?"

Lou began to laugh. He laughed so hard he went into a coughing fit and Mel had to thump his back. But he wouldn't say why he was laughing.

"Joe Isaacs. Number Two Conway Road, the other side of

Market Street. He works shifts, but he's writing a book on Kropotkin, so he's home a lot."

"Grope—who?"

"Just go and see him," said Lou. "He'll tell you what to do when the democratic process fails."

Eleven

Mel and Lucinda, with Ben in attendance, went round to
Conway Road the next evening. Number Two was on the
corner, but it looked like all the others in the terrace, except it
had double glazed windows, the front garden was paved,
and there was a tub with a small tree in it by the front
door.

Lucinda stood back, raising one eyebrow at the tree, while
Mel knocked.

Joe Isaacs was a much younger man than they had
expected. In his early twenties with a thin face, dark penetrating eyes behind glasses with thick frames. He was
wearing jeans and a plaid shirt and didn't look particularly
pleased to see them.

"Lou sent us," Mel said awkwardly, as the others remained silent. He looked them over carefully, not saying
anything, as Mel explained about the litter campaign. "You
know what to do when democracy fails, Lou says."

Joe began to smile.

"It's a waste of time," said Lucinda. "I keep telling her,
but she doesn't take any notice. We could be enjoying
ourselves in the disco, instead of messing with this business. In this crappy place it's a waste of time trying to do
anything."

Joe looked at her, suddenly angry, the smile gone. "Listen,
there are three things you can do if you live in a place like
this. You can accept it and sink to the same level. You can get

out. Or you can change it. But there's a catch there—because to change it, you've got to change yourself first."

There was silence as they took this in.

"Now *you*, Princess—what's your name?"

"Lucinda." Mel heard the irritation in her voice. Her heart sank as she realised that Lucinda was putting up the barriers against Joe already. She could actually feel the tension between them.

"Right. Now then, looking at you, Lucinda Princess, I'd say your solution is to get out. You're after the Big Time. Right? The Good Life? So what is it you want? What do you think you're going to get that's so much better than this?" He gestured at the surrounding houses.

They gaped at him. Lucinda said, stammering, incredulous, "Are you joking? *Money! Clothes! A car!* A really nice *place . . .*"

"So you're going to pawn your life for a fur coat, a few bits of over-stuffed furniture? You think that will give you satisfaction?"

Lucinda was furious at the contempt in his voice.

"Not *furniture*. A better *house*. You think I want to go on living in this stinking hole where everybody hates each other? I want to live in a posher place where you don't keep walking in dog shit, and where you're free to live a decent life. What's wrong with wanting to get out?"

"Woodford? Chigwell? Epping?" asked Joe. "A nice semi-detached where you can't play your stereo after ten without the neighbours phoning the police. Where you get talked about if you don't clean your windows and mow your lawn? You think you'd like people like that?"

"I don't mean some suburban, crappy place like Woodford. I mean a *nice* place."

"Highgate? Hampstead? Chelsea? You think you'd have nice, friendly neighbours in those places? People popping in for a chat and a cup of coffee?"

Lucinda's eyes were flashing with rage.

"You're twisting everything."

"You're the one who's twisted, girl. Twisted up in your values. For God's sake think it out before you smash up your life and it's too late."

"You're out of your mind! What's wrong with wanting money and a car and holidays? Other people . . ."

"Where you going in your big car, Princess? You don't know any good places to go. They'll all be the same to you because you don't know anything. And what you going to do when you've got all the clothes you can cram into your wardrobes? What you going to do when you've made the scene and you're sitting among your furniture in your empty posh flat and you're bored out of your mind with being a sex robot, and there's nothing else you want to buy with all that lovely money? What are you going to do with all that bubbling, foaming brain of yours *then*, Lucinda Princess? You don't look like a religious freak. I'd say it'll be men, then drugs or booze to ease out and forget. You want to do that to yourself?"

Lucinda swallowed, staring at him belligerently, but Mel saw that she was very upset and could not take much more.

"So a Black girl like me can only be happy in a back slum, washing down in the kitchen when no one's around. I'm not supposed to want a bathroom!"

"So it's a *bathroom*, you want!" Joe said derisively.

"We all want bathrooms, Mr Isaacs," Mel broke in angrily. "I think we should have something better than the conditions in these houses. Lucinda's right. It is a slum."

"And whose fault is that? People make slums, they don't just happen. They don't have to accept them. They can change them. You don't have to move to Hampstead to get a bathroom. Come upstairs."

They followed him along the hall. Joe's house was like no other they had ever been in. For a start there was classical music playing somewhere. It seemed empty and spacious. Everywhere was painted a snowy white. There was dark brown carpet on the floors and on the walls were big, brilliantly coloured abstract paintings.

"These are great," said Mel, stopping to look. "Who did them?"

"I did. I'm not an artist, but I like colour and I like to paint."

He went ahead of them upstairs, and at the top flung open a door. They crowded forward to look.

The third bedroom had been converted into a bathroom. A plain white bath. A washbasin. A lavatory. The walls tiled, the floor carpeted in the dark brown. Very simple and plain, but finished with care.

They stared, impressed. Hardly anybody in three streets had a bathroom.

"B . . . but *how*?"

"I did it. I applied for a grant to help with the cost and I saved up. I bought a suite in a sale and I got a book out of the library and learned about plumbing. Then I got a plumber to do the difficult bits. I made a bathroom. Why should I wait for someone else to do it for me? Most of the people could make a bathroom like this if they wanted to, instead of sitting back hoping and moaning."

"I couldn't," Ben broke in, grinning broadly. "I couldn't work out the directions, and my maths are not too hot either. I bet old Mrs Martin would have some trouble humping that bath up the stairs too."

But Joe did not laugh. "Did Mrs Martin ever ask the Council to put in a bath or a shower for her? Make a fuss with the Social Services? I didn't say it was easy, I said, if you want to change things you've got to change your own attitudes first. But that's not your way, is it, man? You don't want to change anything. Your solution is to stay and sink. You don't have to *think*, that way, do you?"

Ben said, easily, "I'm not the brainy type, man. I can't do anything."

"You ever *tried*? Since when did you sit in class and really listen to the lesson?" They heard the contempt again. "Anybody could do anything to you, and you'd let them. They could tell you anything and you'd believe them. Just so everything's nice and easy."

"It's all right for *you*," said Ben. He was angry. Mel couldn't remember the last time she had seen Ben angry. "You gonna come down to the Police Station and pay my fine when they take me in the next lot of riots? *You gonna tell my Mum?*"

"Why don't you lay off, Mr Isaacs," said Mel, angrily. "It's okay for you. Nobody beats *you* up if you're out after eleven. The police don't stop you to search for drugs. Ben's right to stay out of trouble."

"Shut up, *white* girl," said Ben, furious, and went down the stairs, three at a time, slamming the front door.

Joe smiled slowly. "I'm glad to see there's something left after all."

Mel said, upset, "We've been trying to change things, Mr Isaacs. We've really tried, but I've not noticed it having any effect. As Lucinda says, it's a waste of time."

"Is it? You painted your windows and front door didn't you? A red door?"

"Yes, but how . . ."

"I noticed. How many people have painted their houses down your street now?"

"I did Mrs Martin's next door, because she helped me, and she gave me five pounds towards my wallpaper."

"There are five houses painted now. *Five*. The first time there's been any new painting in that road for years. There'll be more. Sometimes it only takes one person. When there's more than one you can move mountains."

Lucinda snorted contemptuously.

"It's true that the men who came to do the gutters said we could become a Redevelopment Area, if we all got together," Mel said, slowly. "Get essential repairs done."

"What's stopping you?"

Lucinda lost her temper. "Redevelopment *crap*! We can't even get our rubbish swept up and you're believing all this garbage he's giving us. We came to see about the litter, *remember*? Haven't we been trying for weeks to change things? Pamphlets. Letters to Councillors. Where have we got? *Nowhere*. They don't take any notice of people like us. You just have to get out as soon as possible. When you've got money, they listen all right."

"What's happened so far?" asked Joe.

They told him about the campaign, and Joe began to grin. It was a very attractive grin, lighting up his serious face and eyes. He's *nice*, thought Mel, surprised.

She said, depressed, "They keep making excuses. Writing lying letters. We don't know what else we can do."

"As it happens, you've come to the right person. I'm an anarchist. No, I don't go round blowing up people. Anarchism is a way of community organisation. No bosses. No parliaments. Mutual responsibility and trust. Direct action." He laughed. "I think we can find a way to solve your little problem."

"Kidnap the Minister of the Environment?" Lucinda sneered.

Joe laughed again. "Not yet. A bit of direct action at the next Council meeting is all that's required."

As they walked down the road Mel said, "Well, what was *that* all about? I've heard of forest fires but that was ridiculous!"

Lucinda grinned at her. "He fancied me and didn't like it."

Mel looked at her, stunned. "You must be joking!"

Lucinda shrugged. "Grow up baby."

93

"You were pretty wild yourself. He really got to you." Mel looked at her sideways. "Seems more like you fancied *him*."

Lucinda put on her haughty African queen look. "I'm only interested in millionaires." They reached the end of the road. "Anyway, he's probably married."

The "direct action" took a little more organisation than Joe had suggested. Like leafleting the four roads once again, calling on dozens of people, sticking reminder notices on the lampposts, and, not least, collecting every bit of rubbish in the roads for two weeks. A lot of people began to get involved.

Ben had talked all the kids in the area into joining the campaign too, and they were able to work a litter rota, twice a day. The rubbish accumulated in black plastic sacks, carefully stored away down the side entrance of the Millers' house, out of sight of curious eyes.

Ben seemed to have changed since the night Joe had picked on him. He was much quieter, and didn't act the clown in the classroom any more. He was so quiet everybody kept asking him if he felt all right. He had even started to do his school work. He told Mel he was sorry for shouting at her, he hadn't meant anything, he was just upset.

"Don't listen to Joe," said Mel. "He likes to get people going."

Ben kicked a lamppost, morosely. "Yeah, but the trouble is, he's right." He slouched off, leaving Mel staring after him.

On the night of the Council meeting, Mel, Lucinda and Ben went along to the Town Hall together. They were secretly worried that something would go wrong at the last minute, that people might have changed their minds, and they would be the only ones to turn up. But they need not have worried.

The entire area, not just their own roads, but relatives recruited from all about, had turned out in force. People were milling around in the floodlights outside the Town Hall. Some of them were even carrying posters and placards.

Mel saw Mrs Ranjit, from Sylvan Street, in her best pink and gold sari, with her old brown coat over the top, shouting and waving a cardboard notice tacked on to a piece of wood.

'WE ARE CITIZENS TOO!' it said. And on the back, 'INDOOR WCS FOR ALL!'

Lucinda looked at the scene, expressionless. "You think maybe we've pushed them a little bit over the top, Mel baby?"

But Mel was excited herself. "Look, the Councillors are coming out. Where is Joe? He's going to be too late!"

But at the exact moment that the Councillors began to come out on to the steps from the meeting, Joe drove through the cheering crowd in a borrowed van. Willing hands unloaded the rubbish sacks and emptied them swiftly. Within seconds the stone steps were awash with the carefully collected stinking rubbish, with some of the choicer items from the railway embankment—two mattresses, a burnt-out cooker, three plastic bowls and a baby's stained carrycot.

The Chairman of the Council, red-faced and furious, was yelling at the single policeman at the door, "Arrest all these people. Arrest them, I tell you!"

There was a good-natured roar of laughter from the crowd as the policeman looked at them helplessly and spread his hands.

"Chairman," shouted Joe. "We've brought the rubbish you said had been collected. We've been doing our own refuse collection and street sweeping. You know where we're going to dump it? On your front garden. There's quite a bit there already. There'll be some more tomorrow. Perhaps they'll collect it from *your* house—they don't collect it from ours!"

"We pay rates too," shouted Mr Miller. "Even if we don't live in Savoy Drive."

"If you've touched my roses . . . you . . . you Rent-a-mob . . . I'll . . ." What he was going to do, nobody heard, there was too much noise. He began to shove through the crowd. "Let me get to my car!"

"You won't get into your garage tonight, love," shouted Mrs Atkins from Blossom Bank Road. "There's a few dumped cars there that need a good home. We've been looking after them for you."

There was another roar of laughter from the crowd.

Mel snorted with laughter. So that's why Tariq Khan had needed an old tow rope, and why the street had looked strangely empty tonight.

"Just see our roads get swept and the rubbish cleared, and you have nothing to worry about," shouted Mr Nicholls. "You might even get re-elected at the May election."

The Chairman got into his car and slammed the door with unnecessary violence, and his wing mirror fell off. Delighted, the crowd burst into cheers and he drove off furiously.

They split up then, pouncing on the other Councillors, who were trying to sneak away quietly.

Afterwards, Mel thought the editorial in the local paper and the pictures of the rubbish on the Town Hall steps had quite a bit to do with the success of the campaign. Whatever it was, within a week, the street sweepers were sweeping daily with their brooms turned the right way up, the bins were being properly emptied, and a special lorry had cleared the rubbish from the railway embankment. The remaining dumped cars had been towed away. The four streets were as clean and empty as a launderette at midnight.

There was public jubilation, and for the first time ever people began to say good morning to each other.

Mel went round to tell Lou all about it—but he was not there and, surprisingly, the shop was shut up, the side gate locked.

Twelve

Mel had no idea how long the junk shop had been closed. The weather had turned bitterly cold and there was ice on the pavements in the morning. Nowadays Keith Edwards often gave her a lift home, so she no longer took the short cut past the shop.

During the next few days she went round specially, but the door remained closed. There must be something wrong. She did not know how to get hold of Mitch, and if he really was *the* Mitch Hamilton, there was no chance at all. He must still be on the road touring, or recording or something.

Then, one afternoon, to her relief, she saw that the shop door was open again, and Mitch was in his usual place, his feet on the desk, looking as disreputable as ever.

"Mitch! Is anything the matter? I haven't seen Lou for ages."

He nodded. "I got back today. I was coming round to see you later. Lou fell down on the ice and broke his leg."

"Broke a leg!" echoed Mel, dismayed. "But that's serious when you're old. Is he in hospital?"

"St Joseph's."

Mel stared at him. She was very upset. She had come to think of Lou as indestructible, something permanent in a shifting tide. She felt stupid. Nothing was permanent. Hadn't she learned her lesson yet?

"Is he all right? I mean, is there anything else?"

"Bored, annoyed, fed up and grouchy as hell," Mitch grinned. "He wants to get out, but they won't hear of it. It'll be a long job. Bones don't heal easily at that age."

"Could I visit him?" asked Mel. "Do you think he'd mind?"

"You're joking. He'd be tickled pink. His visitors aren't exactly queuing up. Just me and old Syd."

"Are you keeping the shop open for him?"

He looked worried. "For a while. When are you going to the hospital?"

She went to see Lou next day. Mitch was there already, sitting on the side of the high hospital bed.

Lou looked surprisingly thin and pathetic in a hospital nightshirt. His old neck, exposed, was corded and scraggy. He had patches of unhealthy colour on his cheekbones and looked uncomfortable with the bedclothes heaped over a frame to keep them away from his leg.

Upset, she looked at Mitch, suddenly glad that he was there. He winked at her encouragingly.

"Well?" said Lou, challengingly. "I'm looking good, aren't I? Handsome as ever?"

"You look terrible," said Mel, bluntly. "How'd you manage to get yourself in here? I told you that beer was too strong for you."

His eyes gleamed with appreciation. "I'm not ready to move on yet, if you've come to say a last goodbye."

"They wouldn't have you. Either place!"

He gave a crack of laughter.

"I've brought you a present." Mel put a couple of cans of beer on the side table out of sight of the nurse, and dropped a copy of *Winning Post* on his bed.

Lou snorted. "Bribery. Don't think I don't know it's Mitch you've come to see."

"How did you guess?" said Mel, coolly. "But he's a better

98

bet, isn't he? You told me—*he's* got all his parts in working order."

Lou said, darkly, "And some of them work a lot more than others."

Mitch got off the bed and shrugged on his sheepskin jacket. He was laughing. "You're a dirty old man, Lou."

"I keep telling you—ro-man-tic. You're going?"

"You know I am. I've got a radio interview. But I'll try to come in on the way to the airport Wednesday."

Mel looked at him curiously. So he was Mitch Hamilton of *Assassination*. It was strange he had never said so.

"Mitch," the old man caught his arm. He wasn't joking now, he looked old and anxious. "You won't let him close the shop down will you? You won't let him sell up while I'm trapped in this dump?"

"He doesn't even know you're in hospital. He'll kill me if he finds out. But you know I've got to close the shop for a bit while I'm in Spain."

"It'll give your father an excuse," Lou said fretfully. Mel thought that for the first time he sounded old, tired. "It's my independence. I won't last a month in a Home."

"Now then, Grandad, don't start that. Nobody's going to close you down."

"*Don't call me Grandad!* Can't we keep it open Saturdays? That'd be better than nothing."

"Look, Grandad, I can't be in two places at once. And who else is there?"

Mel heard herself saying, "What about me? I could open the shop for you on Saturdays."

They both stared at her.

"Well, why not?" said Mel, pushing away her panic. She must be mad. She had never had a job of any kind before, and she was proposing to open a shop all on her own? "What's so difficult? I could keep it open for a few weeks while Mitch is away, if that's what all the trouble is about."

99

The old man's face brightened. "Well, why not! Listen, I'll do a deal. Take out the rent and rates and you can keep the rest of whatever you take."

Mel was annoyed. "I'm helping. I don't need to be paid."

"Independent, aren't we? Don't tell me you couldn't do with a bit of extra cash."

"I could, but I'm not allowed to earn. I'm on Social Security."

"I'll put it away for you. Or maybe there's something you want in the shop. Another armchair?"

Mel wavered. He was looking eager, like a little boy, but so tired and white. She said, reluctantly, "Well, there's this desk . . ."

His eyes gleamed. "Early nineteenth century. Walnut with brass handles. Two hundred and fifty pounds. A snip. Right, it's a deal."

"There's no need. I'll open up for you anyway." She got up.

"You think I'm taking charity?"

Mel smiled at him. "I think you're an obstinate old man. But very generous. Now don't worry about it. It'll be all right."

"The prices . . ."

"Mitch can stick on some labels, or tell me, and if there's anything special I can pop in and ask you, can't I? You're not going anywhere." She grinned at him impudently.

"Just wait. One day they'll look round and I'll be up and out before they can stop me!"

The nurse at the end of the ward smiled at Mel as she trailed out after Mitch. "He looks better. You've cheered him up."

Mel stopped. "Is it all right? I mean, it will heal, won't it? He will be able to walk about?"

The nurse nodded and smiled again. "If it kills him.

Plenty of determination. But it'll take time. Longer than he thinks. Much longer. It's a multiple fracture."

"He looks awful. Shrunken."

"He's old and frail. But he'll get out of here, don't worry."

Mitch was waiting for her outside and they walked down the stone steps and out through the gates to the road. Mel felt depressed. St Joseph's was an old London hospital. Gloomy with stone corridors. The trendy pastel colours and pot plants could not hide its grimness. She shivered. It was almost as bad as Hob's Green.

"You're sure?" said Mitch. "You don't have to do it. It's a thing he has. He doesn't need the money. Hardly any sales anyway."

"It's keeping him going—knowing that he has his own place," Mel said, with certainty. "I need a Saturday job. And there's the desk. I'd do anything for a desk like that."

"Anything?"

"Almost anything!" she amended hastily.

He laughed. "Can you be at the shop tomorrow? I'll start putting the prices on things. I'll be away for four weeks, then another two weeks just after Christmas."

"It's okay. Just let me know when you want me."

Mitch raised his eyebrows, his eyes gleaming. What was the matter with her today? "To open the shop," she said hastily, but it was too late, and she couldn't stop the blush rushing up her cheeks. She turned her head away and heard Mitch laughing.

On Saturday, she got to the shop early. She unlocked the side gate to the yard and the front door with the keys Mitch had given her. There was a queer damp smell, and a lot of others—dirt, mothballs, old polish. It must come from the furniture and other junk, she decided.

She unpacked the sandwiches, coffee, milk and sugar she

had brought with her, made herself a cup on the dirty old gas stove in the back room and sat waiting apprehensively for the customers to arrive. Her first job and she was completely in charge. Her stomach turned queasily.

Two hours and three cups of coffee later, she was still waiting. People passed on the way to the market, but nobody stopped to look in the window even. It was as though the shop was invisible.

At twelve-thirty a man wandered down the side alley, and later came in with two stair posts carved into big acorns at the top.

"How much?"

Naturally, thought Mel bitterly, Mitch hadn't bothered to price the junk in the yard. She had no idea what the posts were worth. "Get what you can," Mitch had said vaguely. How much would *she* be prepared to pay, she wondered, panicking.

She took a chance. "Solid . . . er . . . oak. A snip. Five pounds."

The man took a wallet from his back pocket and gave her ten pounds. He looked pleased. "I've been looking all over for something like these. I'm restoring my house . . . Victorian."

Mel hesitated. She had meant five pounds for the two, but he must know the likely price and he was still looking happy, as though he was getting a bargain. She put the money in the tin cash box.

She chatted with him happily for a few minutes, asking what he had done to his house so far, and swapping hints for cleaning old wood.

Soon after, a small boy with glasses came in to rummage in a box of glass marbles. He said he was buying one each week to make a collection. He knew all about glass marbles and insisted on telling Mel more than she wanted to know about them. He knew how much they cost too, but his eyes shone disturbingly behind his glasses and Mel thought, resigned, that he was probably getting a bargain when he gave her five pence.

After he had gone nothing happened for what seemed like hours and hours. Mel, bored stiff, fell into a daydream, imagining what she would do if she owned the shop herself.

First, she would clean the window so that people could actually see in. Then she would polish up things so they did not look so dusty and dreary. Then she would vacuum up the dirt from the floor. Then, maybe, she would paint the walls a nice pale blue. No—not blue, that made people feel cold, and if they were cold they would not want to buy things. Something cheerful then, to make the furniture look warm and glowing. Peachy-pink, or pale orange. Then she would . . .

"Are you serving, Miss?"

"Sorry," she said, and took fifteen pounds for a small chest of drawers from a man who carried it away in his car. Her best sale so far. She didn't know quite what she had expected from her first job in a shop, but she had certainly not expected to be bored.

But she need not go on being bored. She might as well clean the window, and that horrible gas cooker. She slipped along to the corner shop, careful to take the cash with her, and brought a window cleaning cloth, some dusters, furniture polish and the strongest cooker cleaner she could find.

Two or three customers came in during the afternoon and, at the end of the day, she did her book-keeping in the ledger she found in the bottom drawer of the desk which served as a counter. It had not been used since 1983. Smiling, she turned to a new page and wrote the date at the top and made a list of the things she had sold and added them up. Income: forty-five pounds, five pence. Rent and Rates, thirty-five pounds. Cleaning materials, three pounds, twenty-five pence. Profit, six pounds, eighty pence. Split two ways that made three pounds, forty pence each—three pounds, forty pence for a whole day's work! It just wasn't worth it. Lou could save money by closing the place. But then she remembered his face—old and anxious. "It's my independence," he had said, and Mel knew that it was worth it. There were things more important than money.

But surely there must be a way they could increase the sales? There were some nice things in the shop when you could actually find them. Plates, jewellery. She thought about it all the way home and on and off during the week, as she finished emulsioning the walls of the front room in Cowcross Street.

The following Saturday she got to the shop earlier. She cleaned the window again, thoroughly this time, inside and outside, dusted the furniture she could reach and put some of the china, glass and bits of jewellery in the small window.

In a cupboard in the back room she found an extremely ancient vacuum cleaner, overflowing with clogged dirt, but which, when she emptied it, proved to be still working. She wielded this angrily around the shop and the back room, annoyed that anyone should let the place get so filthy. Men were useless!

The shop was looking better. Already the air of neglect had disappeared. If only there weren't all these boxes and packing cases, stacked all over the place. Packing cases! She thought she had had enough of packing cases to last a lifetime. Nevertheless, she looked inside them curiously. Was Lou packing up an order to go to America? It didn't seem likely somehow. She thought she would pop into St Joseph's on Monday evening and ask him about them.

At first it seemed that all her activity had been a waste of time. Nobody came in, except the man who had bought the stair posts. He poked around for half-an-hour in the yard and emerged, dirty but beaming, with a Victorian cast-iron fire, red with rust.

"I don't know," said Mel, doubtfully. "I'm not sure what it's worth."

"Look," said the man, "They can cost eighty pounds or more, but this is in a bad state. I've got to clean it up and it was buried under piles of junk. I'll give you forty."

"Sixty," said Mel.

"Fifty."

"Done," said Mel. "How do you clean old fires like that? I've got one in my place and I'd like to renovate it."

At lunch time more people stopped to look in the window and to her delight, Mel heard one woman say to another, "It must have been taken over by new people. Let's have a look round on the way back."

In the afternoon more people came in and she was almost busy. Most people bought something, if only to get out of the shop without embarrassment, and at the end of the day when she added up, she found she had ninety-three pounds in the cash box.

Lou said the packing cases were new stock.

"New stock!" Mel said, contemptuously. "Judging by the dirt around them, they've been there for years."

"I've not had time to unpack them yet, have I?" said Lou, righteously, avoiding her eyes. "Very busy I am in that place. I can't get to everything at once."

"Very busy gambling with Syd in the yard," said Mel, severely. "All right, I'll unpack them, but you'll have to price them. I'll bring the things in a few at a time."

"Don't bother," said Lou, hastily. "They're mostly junk boxes I picked up at auctions for next to nothing. China and such like. Get what you can. Charge the same as the other things in the shop. There's a dealers' guide somewhere. I told you, I'm not bothered."

"That's very uneconomic," Mel said, disapprovingly.

"So who are you—that boil on the backside of humanity, the Chancellor of the Exchequer?"

Mel came out of the hospital grinning. He was beginning to sound like his old self.

The following Saturday it was bitterly cold and raining heavily. People put their heads down and hurried past the shop, desperate to get home to the fire and the television. Hardly anyone came into the shop, and the takings were down to fifteen pounds—not even enough for the rent. At this rate she would never earn enough to get the desk.

She stared at it gloomily. She had manoeuvred it into a darker corner and hidden it underneath a huge brass pot, in case someone came in and wanted to buy it. Each time she came to the shop she dusted it lovingly and looked into its mysterious little drawers. It would go beautifully in the alcove by the fireplace in the front room. She could sit there and do her homework as the afternoon sun poured through the front window . . . *If she could sell more things.*

She unpacked three cases, dusted the desk and sat looking at the dirty walls. It was as dreary inside as it was out. Now a nice pink-gold . . . Surely it wouldn't take much effort to emulsion them? She could pull the pieces of furniture a little away from the walls, enough to get her hand down behind them, cover them with polythene . . . It would make everything look so much better, and there was no one coming in anyway.

Before she could change her mind she went along to the cut-price decorators' shop in the next block and bought a can of the paint she had in mind, a thick, once-over emulsion paint.

She went on painting after she closed the shop, and all day Sunday. She put the finishing touches to it Monday evening after school, surprised at how quickly she had done the job. The shop looked so much better that Mel could not believe it herself. Out in the yard she found a worn red stair carpet and, cleaned up, it looked almost luxurious by the door.

She had unearthed a box of plate hangers in the desk. Now she knocked two rows of picture nails into the wall, sorted out a dozen pretty, unchipped plates, washed them in the back room and hung them up. Originally they had all been priced at twenty pence, but they looked so attractive on the glowing wall that she was sure people would be willing to pay more. She took off the price tags and put on others for one pound.

On the back wall she hung up three old mirrors which had been on the floor, tripping her up, and on the side wall she hung all the prints, paintings and frames she could find. Dusted and with the glass polished, they looked interesting and valuable.

She was getting to be an expert on unpacking boxes. Now that there was some sort of order in the shop it was merely a question of cleaning up the things and putting them with the others. There were several silver pieces and vases that looked valuable, together with a lot of small jewellery, medals, silver wine labels, and these she took into Lou and made him set a price on them. She found the dealers' guide Lou had mentioned, and began to learn the approximate value of some of the goods.

She spent some time looking at the antique shop in the High Street, noting how artfully the things had been arranged to look casual, but making the most of the good pieces, showing all the small things close up, arranging larger things inside so they could be seen easily from the window.

On Saturday, the takings were up again. Mel could not believe it was as easy as all that. A woman came in and bought four of the plates from the wall, and Keith Edwards, passing, bought two gilt picture frames and said he would recommend the place to all his friends. Now there was more room, people could actually come in and walk round without falling over things, and there was more to look at anyway.

Mel, locking up, felt really good, but Lou refused to be impressed and said that the takings always went up before Christmas with people wanting chests of drawers and furniture to impress visiting relatives.

That gave Mel another idea. She spent a couple of hours carefully lettering a notice for the window: UNUSUAL CHRISTMAS PRESENTS with a tasteful border of holly leaves.

She covered a couple of boards with hessian and pinned on to them all the brooches, earrings and other bits and pieces of jewellery that she could find. Then she put them in the front of the window. There were some small brass objects too, that she thought might make good presents, some small vases and boxes, some decorated glass. She stacked three sets of china in the window the way she had seen in other shops. She bought some holly and mistletoe from the greengrocers and put it into a large vase at the side of the window.

She remembered then that there was a desk lamp in one of the boxes. Fixed up and hidden by the holly it made a spotlight for the shining china and sparkling silver. She changed the centre lamp too. No wonder the shop had looked dark and dismal—the lamp was only sixty watts.

She looked at the shop from the outside. The whole place looked quite different, cheerful and interesting. Already passers-by were looking in the window. She decided to leave the lamp on all night.

The next day there was a constant stream of customers.

Lou was delighted. "*How* much?" he said, incredulous, looking at the sales listed in the book. "It's seasonal—but it must be something else too."

"Well," said Mel, guiltily, "I had to clean the shop up a bit. I couldn't find anything."

He looked at her suspiciously, gloomily. "What have you been doing to my place? Oh well, I don't suppose it matters.

I'll never go back there now they've got me in this place."

They had moved him to the feared long-stay geriatric ward because he had no one at home to look after him, and even Lou's good spirits had taken a severe blow.

"They can't get me in an old folk's home now," he said. "You have to be able to look after yourself, and they say I need special nursing. I'll never get out of here." There were tears in his eyes.

Mel was alarmed. "Of course you'll get out. You're just depressed. You know it's a long job, but you'll be fit again. I asked the nurse."

He grunted, unconvinced. But he looked more cheerful.

"Here," said Mel, emptying the takings on his bed. "Take a look at this. Two hundred and fifty-nine pounds fifteen pence. I've opened the shop every day this week, as school's broken up. I was just taking it along to the bank."

Lou looked at the small packet of notes and the bag of money. He said, "No, leave it here. I'll see to it."

Mel was surprised. "Okay, but it's no trouble."

"Come on, tell me all about it." He sounded surprisingly cheerful now. "What have you got rid of?"

Thirteen

The day before Christmas Eve Mel went to see her mother in Hob's Green. Her mother looked plumper and prettier. She was wearing lipstick and someone had cut her hair into a fashionable short style which suited her. But she was twisting her hands and looked lost and anxious, less calm than when Mel had seen her last. When she opened the present Mel had bought for her—a plain woollen dress in a clear turquoise, which had once been her favourite colour, she started to cry and would not stop.

Mel stood up and watched her helplessly.

"It's all right," she said, trying desperately to keep talking, "I've been working, saving up. I hope it fits . . . I wasn't sure . . ." And then a nurse came and hurried her away.

Mel got on the bus feeling ill and depressed, and stared unseeingly out of the window. It all seemed so hopeless. What was she working for?

Instead of going home she turned off to Lou's shop. It was still early. She could sort out some more things for the window and clean up ready for tomorrow. One more shopping day to Christmas. Some Christmas. She felt too miserable to want to join in a happy family party. Mrs Miller had prepared enough food to feed the whole street.

"What are you doing for Christmas, Mel?" Keith Edwards had asked at the end of term. Mel's heart had leapt. Perhaps he was having a party. Was he going to suggest that she should call in to see him?

She shrugged. "I'm working in the shop Christmas Eve. I want to earn as much as possible. I'm saving up for a desk."

"I'll be calling in," Keith said. He smiled into her eyes. "Don't go away."

Mel's heart lifted, remembering. He hadn't been in so far, so she would be seeing him tomorrow, and maybe, just maybe, he would invite her to spend Christmas Day with him.

As she was making coffee in the shop she heard a key fitting into the door. It was Mitch, staring around incredulously.

"Mitch! What are you doing home? I thought you were in Spain."

"We got homesick. Thought we'd fly back, just for Christmas. What on earth have you done to the old shop, Mel? I thought I'd come to the wrong place."

Mel said, annoyed. "Cleaned up all the muck you both left. Don't say thank you."

He laughed and came over to her. "I'm not criticising. I think it's great."

"The takings are up. More tomorrow, fingers crossed. I'll have enough for my desk soon."

"Listen, Mel, what are you doing for Christmas?"

"Nothing special. I'll be at the Millers'. What am I supposed to be doing? She's still inside. I saw her today. I thought she was getting better but it will be *months* . . ."

Suddenly she was crying and Mitch was holding her and kissing her gently. "Mel, we'll have our own party. How's that? At your place. We'll have Barney and his girl and Pete, if he's free . . . and your friend Lucinda . . ."

"No, I don't think . . ." What was the matter with her? It would be fun. She always felt all right with Mitch—but suppose Keith was going to ask her to spend Christmas Day with him and she couldn't go? She pulled away from Mitch.

"There isn't any food, and I'm not sure . . ."

"Try not to sound too enthusiastic," said Mitch, sharply. He looked at her penetratingly. "What about your teacher? He's got a party going maybe? He's seen you're fixed up?"

Mel coloured and walked away to make more coffee.

Mitch said, "So that's it. You're waiting for him to suggest something."

"No I'm not! I just don't feel like parties right now."

Mitch came over and put his arms around her and rubbed her cheek with his. "I've missed you, Mel. Look, I don't really want any parties either. Just you and me."

"I told you, there isn't any food," Mel said, annoyed. He was sorry for her, and she did not want anybody's pity. "I'll be all right. I don't need anybody looking after me, thanks all the same. You know there are stacks of places you'd rather be."

Mitch kissed her, laughing, and sat down. "Okay, let's make a shopping list. I'll go round Sainsbury's tomorrow and get the stuff."

Mel looked at him. "Are you crazy? You can't. You'll be recognised and you'll need the police to get you out."

He looked suddenly dejected. "Oh hell, I forgot." Then a slow colour crept under his cheek bones. "You know."

"Why didn't you tell me?"

"I told you I was in a band."

"You didn't tell me it was Assassination and you'd had these hits, and that you're a star."

He shrugged and looked away. "People change towards you when you get a hit. They start thinking you're something special. How did you find out?"

"There was a picture of you in the fanzine that was going round school last term."

"You didn't say anything." He looked at her curiously and sat down, hunched, on the kitchen chair.

"Well, I might have made a mistake, and then I thought you might want to be private."

Mitch said quietly, "This shop, Cowcross Street, they are the only places I feel like myself. It was all right when we were gigging. Fun on the road, and playing the music, but all this bullshit since we made the big time—I can only stand so much. I'm having trouble handling it. Fame isn't so marvellous in some ways. I need to get back here to keep my head together. It's real here and people take you just as you are. No hype. No hangers-on."

Mel gave him a cup of coffee and pushed the sugar over to him not saying anything.

"I should have explained."

She shrugged. "Well, it's your business. Nothing to do with me."

He slapped the cup back on its saucer and got up. "Not bloody interested either, are you?"

Mel looked surprised. "What have I said? Are you suffering from jet lag or something?"

He was angry. "I'm fine! Well, what about Christmas then?"

"No thanks. Mrs Miller would be upset. And anyway," she just remembered, "what about Roxy Leigh?"

"*Roxy?*" He stared at her blankly.

Mel was embarrassed. "Well, I mean, these last few weeks there have been all these newspaper stories about you and Roxy Leigh, the singer. I thought . . . I mean, it seems like you're, er, very good friends. It's nothing to do with me, but I would have thought you'd want to be with her . . ."

Mitch was furious. "I don't know what the hell you're on about. I'm not with Roxy Leigh! But you're right about one thing, Roxy is nothing to do with you—so mind your own business."

He went out, slamming the door, leaving Mel staring after him.

Christmas Eve was her best day of trading so far. Mel took

nearly eighty pounds and was constantly busy. Mitch appeared around lunch time, muttering an apology for his bad temper.

"I'd like to talk to you about Roxy, some time, Mel."

"That's okay," Mel said, watching him warily. "You were right. I should keep out of other people's business." She smiled at him politely. He hadn't seemed the moody type when he was working on the dresser, but he was certainly a lot more sensitive than she had thought. She hardly knew him, after all, and he was a big star. Maybe he was temperamental. She smiled at him politely again, but he stared back at her gloomily, and after helping with a sudden rush of customers, took himself off to visit Lou in hospital.

It was not until later in the afternoon when the shop emptied, that she realised that Keith Edwards had not come in as he had promised. She watched the hands of the clock move round, and at last was forced to admit that he was not coming. She stayed open an extra half-hour, but he still did not appear and she locked up sadly and put his Christmas present back in her bag. She had found a little silver snuff box among the small objects in the shop. It had a small painting on the front of a smiling man in brown velvet looking rather like Keith. It had cost her five pounds, and cheap at the price, as Lou had said when she insisted on paying for it, but even so, it was a lot of money for her.

Perhaps Keith had forgotten his promise? She couldn't bring herself to believe that. Something important must have happened to stop him. An *accident* even? Her heart flipped over and she felt sick.

She walked home quickly, trying not to worry. It was stupid—*anything* could have stopped him. But later in the evening she gave in, pulled on her jacket, put his present in her pocket and found herself walking towards Keith's flat.

There were a lot of smart cars parked nearby, and she saw

114

that the large bay window of his ground floor flat was brightly lit, the curtains open.

Her heart banging, she stood across the road and looked in. There were silver and gold decorations and a light flashing in time to the disco music flooding loudly across the pavement. The room was crowded with dancers. A pretty girl in a tight dress with no back shimmied into the room with a plate of mince pies held above her head. Then suddenly, Mel saw Keith. He was wearing dark jeans and a black satin shirt, his fair hair shining. He looked so handsome that her heart contracted. He pulled a sprig of mistletoe from behind his back with a flourish and held it over the girl's head. He was laughing.

Mel turned away abruptly and almost ran down the street.

Mel ate a huge Christmas dinner with the whole Miller clan and watched television with them, but later she needed desperately to get away by herself for a while.

"Why don't you go for a walk? Get some exercise?" said Mrs Miller, casually. And Mel knew that she understood. Sometimes she seemed to understand what Mel felt even before Mel did.

The streets were deserted; the frosty air so clear she could see the stars.

Maybe her mother was nervous and ill because they were cutting down her drug dosage, which was good news really. As for Keith, she could see that he had been much too busy with arrangements for his party to bother about coming into the shop. There was no need to be so upset. He would explain next term. It would have been nice to be invited to the party too, but after all, she was only one of his pupils, and why should he think of her as someone special?

She would go on with the work of redecorating Number Six. There was no need to be discouraged; she had come a long way and her mother would be better one day. In the meantime, she would start stripping the torn wallpaper off the passage and staircase.

She found that Mitch had put an envelope through her door. There was a card with a sad-looking cat with holly drooping behind its ear, saying, "I'm sorry—anybody can make a mistake!" and inside, "Why didn't they tell me turkeys aren't yellow?"

Mel laughed and opened the tissue paper wrapping inside.

A delicate silver chain bracelet fell into her palm. 'A present from Spain,' Mitch had written, 'See you in the New Year.' It was beautiful, the best present anybody had ever given her, but Mel felt uncomfortable. It was *too* good. After all, she hardly knew him, and there was his girlfriend. She wondered what Roxy Leigh would say if she knew.

Fourteen

Mitch completed his tour and came back in mid-January. He was stretched out, feet up on the desk, looking red-eyed and dissipated, when she went round to the shop one afternoon after school.

"I've got another job for you, Mel."

"Yeah, sure you have," she said, warily. He seemed different somehow, older, more confident, and fizzing with some secret amusement.

"No messing about. Straight up."

"Dust your limo? Freeze your whisky?"

"You don't freeze whisky," he said, scandalised. "Lager."

"Brush your coat then?"

His eyes gleamed appreciatively. "Now that's not a bad idea. Personal dresser, how's that? You can help me out of my pants after the show."

"I thought the groupies did that!"

"Don't tell me you're jealous already."

"Grinding my teeth," said Mel, absently. She had found the box she was looking for. China oddments, mostly chipped or broken. There had been a Victorian sauce boat without its lid, with lovely curvy lines like Aladdin's lamp. Last night, in bed, she had thought of just the use for it. On the mantelpiece in the front room, with a trailing plant in it. Mrs Martin would give her a piece of tradescantia. To her pleasure it was still there. She pulled it out and rubbed the

117

dirt off with her sleeve. It had a nice gold band, and scattered pink rosebuds.

"Twenty-five pence. Everything in that box twenty-five pence," said Mitch, grinning.

"It's a robbery," said Mel. "Look, it's got a chip at the bottom."

"Twenty-pence, then, to a regular customer. What about it then?"

"Yes, it's nice. I'll have it."

He breathed exasperatedly. "I meant, what about my offer?" He sounded embarrassed.

She looked at him. "What offer?"

He groaned. "Not even listening. You realise that some girls hang on my every word?"

"Like maggots?" She saw then that he was getting annoyed. She sat on a brass coal box, propped her chin up with one hand and looked at him with wide, soulful, adoring eyes. To her surprise he went bright red and looked away.

"Well, go on. I'm hanging."

"No, it doesn't matter. You'll just joke and this is important."

Moody. She had had enough of moody, screwed-up people. She shrugged, got up, found a piece of crumpled newspaper in the back room, and began to tuck it around the sauce boat.

He said abruptly, "Where are you going?"

"Where do you think? *Home*, to do my homework. I've got about three hours of it, and the Mocks start next week. It's not Saturday."

"Look, I want you to come to a party with me. A kind of party."

Mel stared at him, her mouth hanging open. He *was* crazy. Crazy or joking. But he wasn't joking. In fact he had gone red again. That made twice in one day.

"What's the matter? Nobody asked you to a party before?" He sounded irritable.

"Only the school disco," said Mel, incurably honest. "A *girl*. Not a pop star with a record in the charts."

She sat down on the coal box again and looked at him narrowly. "Okay, you might as well spill it. I don't look like Janey Adams or Roxy Leigh, so it's not that you fancy me."

The Assassination fanzine had said that these were his favourite females. She looked sideways at him and was startled to see the colour deepening under his cheek bones. He must be sick!

She was relieved to hear him laugh. "That's what I like about you, Mel. You've got all your marbles and they work overtime. Look, it's like this. I've got to go to a reception to promote our new album. We've gone gold, and there's a presentation."

"Great!" said Mel. "So what's the problem?"

"I have to take a girl along. The right girl. Everyone there will have his old lady, or his girlfriend, except me. I haven't got a girl."

Mel stared at him, disbelieving. "Aw, come on, you must know dozens of girls."

"Not the sort I'd want to take to a champagne party with the President of my record company. Pearl-grey shantung suit, and an acknowledged expert on Vivaldi."

"Serves you right for having low tastes."

"We've only just hit the big time," he protested. "We've been gigging for years. Up and down the bloody motorway. Now there's recording sessions, promotions, interviews—I haven't had time to chat up nice girls. All I meet are boilers and a few fans, and then we move on. I need an intelligent girl who can talk nicely to all these fat cats without grovelling, screaming like a hyena, or making them ask themselves what kind of guy I am to pick *that* up."

Mel ignored the implied compliment. She said bluntly,

119

"Why don't you take Roxy Leigh? A star like that ought to be good for your status."

He looked embarrassed and ran his fingers through his hair. "Yes, well, er, there's a little problem there."

"She seems to like you a lot. There are all these pictures in the paper, and they keep hinting she's going to marry you."

"*She* keeps hinting she's going to marry me. And I don't want her getting any more wrong ideas." His voice rose.

"All right, calm down." She grinned. "There's no need to get panic-stricken."

"That's all you know."

"Yes, well, maybe you'll have time to look around."

"I have looked around and I'm asking *you*."

"Where is this shindig taking place?"

He hesitated, watching her. "The Rochester."

Mel burst out laughing. She got to her feet, slid the sauce boat into her plastic carrier, still laughing. "Can you see me at the Rochester?"

"Yes," he said, not laughing. "What's so funny?"

"My mum's in the nuthouse. I'm living on Social Security in a back-street slum. I'm still at school and I look a mess. That's what's funny."

"You'd be fine with the right clothes and your hair done."

Suddenly, unexpectedly close, he reached for her and pulled off the elastic band she used to keep her hair back. He smoothed her hair softly over her forehead and round her face, looking at her intently. "You'd look better with a few curls. I like girls with curly hair."

She jerked her head away from his hands. "You're crazy. What am I supposed to go in? A tee shirt and my school skirt?"

"I'll buy you an outfit, of course." He was impatient.

She said angrily, "If you think . . ."

"Look, it's a *job* I'm offering you. I'll pay you twenty pounds to come and be my partner for the evening, plus a hairdo, plus a dress, shoes, bag—whatever you want."

She stared at him. "You really mean this, don't you. But *why*? Why me? It's crazy."

"No it's not. I trust you Mel. You won't get wrong ideas, and you won't talk about it to anyone. You've known for weeks I help out here in the shop, and you've not told a living soul as far as I can see, otherwise they'd all have been round to look at me, like a goldfish. You've got a quiet voice and you're not impressed with famous names."

"It's *no good*, Mitch. I don't know how they go on in places like the Rochester."

"Neither do I. We can both find out."

"No, I'm sorry. I'm a coward. I'd show you up."

"Twenty pounds. A hairdo. A dress. And *the desk*."

"The desk?" She looked back at him, her eyes bright with suspicion. "It's going to be an expensive evening for you," she said, slowly. "It must be very important to spend that kind of money."

She was caught, she knew. *The desk*. She couldn't turn down an offer like that. Not with the desk thrown in. But there had to be something he wasn't telling her.

"Forget the money," he said, impatiently. "There's plenty of money. It *is* important to me. And you want the desk. I can see it now in your front room in the alcove next to the fireplace. All the little brass handles gleaming. It'd look great. Isn't it worth it? Just for spending a few hours with me? I'm not a bad bloke. You might even enjoy it." His voice changed. "I helped *you* with your dresser."

"All right. There's no need to use blackmail. I'll do it."

He took a deep breath. "That's great."

She could feel the surge of his excitement. It made her even more worried.

"The evening ends when we leave the party, right?" Better

to have everything clear. Rock and roll bands were notorious for their free and easy ways.

"We might go on to a club."

"When we leave the club then."

He looked at her, expressionless. "If you say so."

"When is it?"

"Next Thursday."

He pulled a roll of notes from the back pocket of his old denims and counted out some ten pound notes. There seemed to be plenty left, Mel thought, relieved.

He tugged the hair that was falling loosely over her eyes. "Don't forget. Little curls."

"How do I know what kind of dress to buy?"

"Something soft, clinging . . ." He grinned at her expression. "*Pink*. Don't worry, I'll come with you."

"It's all right," said Mel, hastily. "I'll ask Lucinda. She works at a boutique in Covent Garden. She knows what's fashionable."

"Fine. We'll go there."

Mel could not think of a way to tell him she did not want him along, especially as he was paying, and in the end Mitch went with her, lounging on the leather seat of the boutique and exchanging flip jokes with Lucinda, who had been sworn to secrecy.

Her worst misgivings were realised. They chose for her a silk jersey suit of deep rose colour with a belt, full sleeves and a band of hand embroidery around the deep cut neckline.

"No, I don't think this is right," Mel said desperately, wondering how she was going to find the courage to wear it. "It's too low cut, and it sort of clings . . ."

"Look, *dummy*," said Lucinda, impatiently, forgetting Mitch. "Time to grow up. It's *supposed* to cling. It's supposed to show off your outstanding assets. I told you, that's your bum and your ti . . ."

"All *right*!" shouted Mel, "There's no need . . ."

"If you've got it, baby—*flaunt it!*" Lucinda quoted throatily, winking at Mitch behind Mel's back.

He said, grinning, "Honestly, Mel, that's the one. You look marvellous."

"And here's the bag and the sandals that go with it."

"But I can't walk on heels that high," Mel's voice squeaked.

"Walk? Who's walking? It's the Rochester and a limo, baby. Not the Rose and Crown. Anyway you can practise." She wrapped them up and put them with the suit into one of the boutique's glossy shoppers. "Come on, now you need a hairdresser. Three doors along. I'll introduce you to Evelyn."

Evelyn turned out to be a macho young man with exceptionally tight jeans, who beamed all sorts of messages at Mel's eyes in the mirror to her intense embarrassment. But she had to admit that he knew his job. Her too-heavy fringe was cut away and curved into tendrils and wisps, with a deep sexy wave over one eye, and the long tails of her hair were shaped away into her neck.

Back in Cowcross Street, Lucinda walked round her, grinning. "Well, you still wouldn't make *Gold Rush*. But you might make *Just Seventeen*." She walked round her again. "You might even make *The Face*. I reckon I did a really good job on you. Maybe I ought to go into the model agency business!"

Mitch did not say much. Just, "You look good". But the look in his eyes had Mel wondering uneasily if she had done the right thing in agreeing to go to the party with him.

Fifteen

They went to the promotion party in Mitch's new car—low and sleek and very, very expensive.

Mel had worried about arriving at the hotel, walking through the big imposing doors, insecure on the high heels, sure she would feel lost and not know what to do. But she found it was easier to walk on the heels than she thought, and when the car drew up, the doorman stepped forward and opened the car door, ushering them quickly and discreetly into the hotel foyer. There a girl from the record company swooped on them, took the special passes from Mitch, and wafted them into a silent lift up to the suite where the reception was well under way.

Mel looked round the crowded room apprehensively. Now came the awful part. She hoped she would not have to talk to many people. There were so many more than she had thought. She ought not to have come. What on earth was she going to talk about?

She said, panicking, "Everyone looks so fantastic."

Mitch shrugged and put his arm around her shoulders, drawing her into the room. "Liggers."

"Liggers?"

"Hangers-on, out for a freebie."

"But I recognise some of them. They're famous! Look, there's Janey Adams!"

"They're with the company. What are you worried about? You look pretty fantastic yourself."

Mel smiled at him reluctantly. "You don't look so bad either. I hardly recognised you without the old trainers, the split jeans and the tee shirt."

Mitch grimaced. "I feel a fool in a suit."

"Wow!" said Mel, "Who's *that*?"

Across their line of sight drifted a vision of elegance. A very tall, thin man, dressed from head to foot in shades of pale grey. Grey silk shantung suit, grey silk shirt, silver grey suede shoes, grey bow tie, and grey silk hanky, folded into his top pocket. Silver hair. Even his skin looked grey, Mel thought. He was moving in a kind of royal progress slowly around the room, shaking hands absent-mindedly with the guests, attended at a short distance by two earnest executives in dark grey suits and dark glasses.

"Mr St Clair, the President of the record company," said Mitch. "My boss."

"The Vivaldi expert?"

"You've got a good memory."

"Who are the others?"

"Boot-lickers," said Mitch, succinctly.

A voice immediately behind them said, "Thank Christ you got here at last, Mitch. I've been in a right two-and-eight."

He was pale, with high cheek bones and gorgeous dark auburn hair curling in a great mane to his shoulders. His eyes were brilliant blue, clear and saintly.

"This is Barney, our drummer," said Mitch. He sounded wary. "He's—um—my special buddy. We were at school together."

Mel smiled at him, and Barney looked her over and breathed out reverently, "Class. Definitely *class*. You've kept her dark, you crafty sod. You didn't pick her up at one of our gigs!"

Mitch winced. "Where's Pete?"

Barney shrugged. "Not here. I reckon he's chickened."

"But he can't," said Mitch, alarmed. "He's accepting the award. I'm not doing it."

"Do you want to bet?"

Mitch said, "Did you bring anyone Barney?"

Barney jerked his thumb over his shoulder. Against the wall, sitting on the very edge of a gilt chair, there was a very young girl with a terribly vacant expression. She was rather grubby, in a short black satin skirt, and white satin shoes that clearly belonged to her older sister.

"God, *Barney* . . ."

"Yeah, well, I didn't have time to find anyone, and I woke up with her this morning, so I thought I might as well kill two birds . . ." Barney's blue eyes beamed angelically at Mel. "See, you haven't got time to be fussy in this business, and her *hands* were clean. I always look at their hands as well as . . ."

Mitch said, hurriedly, "Barney, where's Malc? He's our manager—he can accept the award!"

"He's in the Men's Room, putting Johnny's head under the tap. He's stoned out of his mind. Thinks he's come to play a gig at Sheffield City Hall. It's the only way we could get him into the limo."

Mitch groaned, looking harrassed. "Honestly, Mel, we're not really as bad as we sound."

Barney nodded. "Terror. Sheer terror. That's what's done for him. All these fat cats and chandeliers. None of us wanted to come. I've hardly been out of the lavatory since I got here and Mitch is frightened that Roxy Leigh will get him."

"Roxy!" Involuntarily Mitch glanced over his shoulder in a hunted way, which made Mel laugh again.

"It's all right. She's not here—yet." Barney said.

Mitch groaned again. "Excuse me, Mel. I'm going to get Malc, just in case."

"What is all this about Roxy Leigh?" Mel asked Barney,

curiously. "I thought they were practically getting married."

Barney shook his head. "Not if he can help it. He's terrified of her. She's been chasing him for the last six months. All over the country. Leeds. Birmingham. Glasgow. Turning up backstage unexpectedly. You know, when we're off the road he can't use his flat? She arrives in the middle of the night, banging up the neighbours . . ."

So that was why Mitch spent so much time in Lou's shop. Mel said, "But can't he just tell her he isn't interested—if he isn't?"

Barney laughed. "*Tell* her? He's told her till he's blue in the face. He's written letters. He's phoned her. The things he's done to get out of her way! Crawled out of the loo window at Hammersmith. Got out of the Ipswich Gaumont in a blond wig. Malc's told her. *I've* told her. She doesn't take any notice. Somewhere or other she's got hold of the idea that he's shy and retiring, and she knows he hasn't got a girl. Honest, Mel, in this business you meet blokes who are ego-maniacs, but believe me, they've got nothing on Roxy Leigh. Man, she just knows she knows everything. She can get anything she wants. Poor old Mitch!"

He began to laugh again, doubling up. "There was the time . . ."

Mel saw that Mitch had rejoined them, still looking nervously over his shoulder. "Malc's getting some black coffee for Johnny."

"Hey, Mitch, what about that time in—where was it—Grimsby? Roxy got him trapped in the dressing room by himself and we suddenly heard these shouts—'Help! Help!'"

"Look, Barney . . ."

"You know we all thought it was maybe some nutter who was trying to do him in for pinching his girlfriend or something, so we broke the door down. We were all there—the band, the roadies, the lighting crew. Right, Mitch?"

"Yes," he said, sourly. "But there's no need . . ."

"And there was Roxy, waving Mitch's jeans round her head, kind of stalking him, and there he was, dodging round the room clutching a towel to his front, screaming his head off like a Victorian maiden."

Mel began to laugh.

"Very funny," said Mitch, bitterly. "Thanks a bundle, Barney, *old friend*. That's a real good story to tell my girl."

Barney caught his eye and tried to straighten his face. "It's okay, Mitch. It didn't mean anything. Look, Mel's *laughing*. It's not as though you were fu . . ."

"*Shut up*, Barney!" Mitch said, dangerously. "Look, why don't you go find a nice quiet cage somewhere?"

". . . like that time in . . ."

"I'm going to *kill* you in a minute, Barney."

Intrigued, Mel said, "What time?"

"Well, Mitch has this thing about Catfish Hodge . . ."

But before Mel could hear the Catfish Hodge story, there was a commotion over by the entrance. Heads turned, conversation ceased.

First came a very handsome young man in a smart chauffeur's uniform, leading a beautiful Afghan hound, with long delicate legs and keen eyes.

"Roxy!" said Barney. "She goes everywhere with that dog. It's her latest status symbol."

The chauffeur handed the lead to the man following him, plump, with a moustache. Roxy's manager? He then stood back and made a deep bow as Roxy Leigh herself came through the door, posing on the threshold and gathering all eyes.

"Oh my God," said Mitch.

She was wearing tight leather pants, a tiny white tulle ballet skirt, high stiletto-heeled boots hung with chains and a huge, studded bomber jacket. Under it, the gathers of her tight scarlet satin blouse strained across her splendid bosom, the neck plunging to her waist, aquiver with black maribou feathers. Her face was a dead white mask, the eyes rimmed in double green and black lines which were taken out under her brows like enormous spectacles. Her lips were purple, and her long talons were painted black. Her hair stood away from her head, stiffened into short green spikes, and on top sat a small flowered hat with a spotted veil.

She put her hand on her hip and surveyed the room moodily.

"Hi, Roxy," said someone, casually, standing by the door. She ignored the greeting. Her eyes roved the room, rested balefully on Mitch, who paled visibly, and then moved on to Mr St Clair, who, innocent and unaware, had arrived to chat in a fatherly way with Barney.

Roxy's throaty, penetrating voice knifed across the room. "Felix, baby!"

Once more, the heads turned, this time with incredulous delight. Roxy stalked down the room towards them, in that curious undulating way, which sent her fans wild.

Mr St Clair turned slowly, hardly believing, and stared at her, his eyes protruding. One of the executives leaned close and hurriedly whispered in his ear. Mr St Clair nodded and looked grim.

"Good evening, Miss . . . er . . . Leigh, isn't it?"

"Oh don't be so frigid, Felix, honey. I've been dying to see you. There's been a terrible misunderstanding about my new contract."

Mr St Clair, glacial, said, "Miss Leigh, this is not the place . . ."

"Aren't we the stuffed shirt! Look, buster, I've been trying to get at you for a week and you've been too busy, so what better time . . ."

"*Next week*, Miss Leigh, not *now*."

129

"Who the hell do you think you are—refusing to see *me*? You know how much money I've made for your poxy record company?"

Her manager began to chatter hysterically into her ear.

Mr St Clair, dignified, turned his back majestically, dismissing her.

"We have some splendid, um, eccentrics in the music industry have we not?" he said to Barney and Mitch.

One of the grey-suited minions stepped forward hastily and introduced Mitch and Barney to him.

"Ah yes, the honoured guests. I believe it is your group, um, Assassination, which we have come here to toast today. I am to present an award to you later on."

"Not to me, to Pete Lloyd," said Mitch. "But yes, I'm with Assassination."

"They tell me your record has, um, gone gold, as they say. A splendid achievement. Splendid. We of the company salute you."

"Cheers," said Barney.

"And this charming young lady with the extraordinary eyes, she too is one of the group?"

Mel laughed. "I can't sing a note."

Mr St Clair sighed. "Not at all unusual today, my dear. Don't worry about it."

"I mean I'm not . . ."

"Michael! *Honeybird!*"

Out of the corner of her eye, Mel saw Roxy advancing, her arms wide apart, a big glass of red wine in one hand.

"Baby Wassums!"

Mitch did not look round. He said, evenly, "This is Melody Calder, Mr St Clair . . ."

"Mickey darling! *Sweetiebums!*"

Mel caught Barney's eyes, and choked, trying desperately to turn it into a cough. Mitch, his ears scarlet, glanced at her briefly, furious, and looked back at Mr St Clair. His voice rose, clear, decisive. "Mel Calder, Mr St Clair, my fiancée. We're getting married soon."

There was a choked scream behind them.

"Michael, *sweetheart*, what are you *saying*?" Roxy's cry echoed over the polite chatter.

Mel, stunned herself, saw Roxy go rigid, her eyes dilate, her fingers tighten on the glass, and was already half-prepared, when, without more hesitation, Roxy threw the glass and its contents straight at her. Mel stepped back hastily, the glass sailed by her nose and arrived, a bull's eye, in the centre of Mr St Clair's beautiful shantung jacket.

"Miss Leigh!"

He stepped back, cowering behind his hands, expecting another attack, and trod on the Afghan hound sitting politely next to Roxy's manager. The dog gave an outraged howl, jerked his lead from the manager's inert hand, and tore off around the room, yelping.

A young man by the door lunged to catch him as he passed, lead trailing, but the dog swerved, the young man lost his balance and slid neatly across the feet of a waiter coming through the door with a full tray. The drinks rose slowly into the air and descended in an arc over the guests by the door. There were indignant screams, laughter, shouting.

It was at this point that the cat made its presence known.

It was picking its way with insufferable arrogance along the beautifully spread buffet table.

The Afghan hated cats. With a howl of rage the dog leapt for it, pawing at the tablecloth and dragging it down. The dishes cascaded over the side like a waterfall. The cat, with a derisive yowl, jumped for safety on to the highest point it could see, which, unluckily, happened to be Mr St Clair's shoulder. With its claws well dug into his neck and shoulder, it hissed a series of bloodcurdling challenges at the dog. The dog, incensed, jumped again for the cat, missed, and by way of compensation, sank its teeth deep into Mr St Clair's wrist.

Roxy tottered, fainting, towards Mitch. He lowered her hastily to the floor, not noticing the scattered serving forks. With a howl to rival the dog, she sprung up again, clutching her bottom and stamping her stiletto heels into Mr St Clair's suede-covered toes.

Total chaos reigned everywhere.

Mel and Barney were hanging on to each other, hysterical with laughter. Mel, her stomach aching, was desperately trying to get control so that she could breathe properly. But the sight of Mitch guiltily trying to find out exactly where Roxy had been injured sent her off again.

Mr St Clair was now staggering around in small circles making tiny hooting noises, trying to shake off the dog and cat, and hold his toes. His executives watched him, transfixed with horror. The red wine dripped redly down his jacket, over his hand . . .

Mel sobered suddenly, realising that not all the dripping red was wine. Some of it, an increasing amount, was *blood*. The dog had bitten him rather badly and torn the skin. Surely the minions could see he was bleeding? Someone —anyone—ought to do something.

The Afghan had remembered its original grudge against Mr St Clair's feet and began worrying his ankles, while Mr St Clair did a bouncing pogo to keep him away.

Mel gulped, feeling the laughter welling again. Somebody *had* to do something. The executives were in a catatonic trance. She stepped forward and picked up the Afghan's lead.

"*Bad* dog," she said. "Sit."

The animal looked at her, surprised and hurt.

"*Sitttt.*" Mel hissed. "*Sittttt!*" This time the dog sat. Mel gave the lead to Roxy's manager. "Get it out of here, quick," she said, her voice wobbling with suppressed laughter.

The dog was dragged off barking, protesting. Mel said to

the cat, "Come on down, Pussy. Poor Pussy. He's all gone."
The cat batted her hands away contemptuously with a
paw of open claws and sprang to a lower level—Roxy's
head—on its way to the floor. Its claws caught in the spotted
veiling of Roxy's hat.

"Get it off," shrieked Roxy, shaking her head violently. "I
hate cats. Get off you mangy fleabag!"

The cat, losing its balance, leapt for the table, taking with
it Roxy's hat, and not only the hat. Attached to it still was a
spiky green wig. Roxy suddenly looked surprisingly bald, her
head covered with mouse-coloured fuzz.

Barney, whooping with laughter, sounded as though he
was having an attack.

The cat, annoyed, disentangled its claws, selected a
chicken breast and retired with it under the table.

Mel, her voice shaking, said, "Come along, Mr St Clair,
it's time to go."

He stared at her, dazed. His pale blue eyes looked exactly
like the dog, hurt and stunned, not believing what had
happened to him. He held out his wounded wrist, his face
crinkling like a small boy about to cry. Mel's health education lessons began to flick over in her mind. Bleeding *and*
shock. Staunch bleeding, loosen clothing, warmth, rest. She
swallowed a sudden attack of panic, took his hand and led
him to the door, talking to him soothingly.

"Poor Mr St Clair. It's all over now. You'll soon be all
right. You must lie down to recover, until your car is brought
round."

"Animals!" he said, petulantly. "These people are animals. Never again will I promote a pop record. *Never*. No
matter what they say. Roxy Leigh must go. They must all
go . . ."

"You're upset. Tomorrow everything will look different.
It's been a nasty experience for you. There, there . . ."

At the doors stood a man in an evening suit, wringing his

hands. The hotel manager, thought Mel, relieved. Some-body sane.

"Mr St Clair needs a room to lie down in. He is very shaken," she said, loudly, and as Mr St Clair tottered on through the gaping hotel staff gathering around the door, she hissed, "And get a doctor up there *fast*. He's bleeding."

"Bleeding!" The manager was outraged. "We don't have bleeding in this hotel." He clapped his hands. "Mr Hinkson? Boy!"

"A doctor, or you may have a corpse as well," Mel advised, kindly, and tried to keep her face straight, as the manager, his back rigid with disapproval, led the way to the lift. Mr St Clair held on to her hand pathetically.

"I should have known," said the manager, bitterly, stab-bing the lift button. "Bleeding. Corpses. I was advised not to have these wild rock men in my hotel." He stared angrily at Mr St Clair.

Mel coughed to choke the laughter, and turned to the trotting executives.

"*You*—wrap him in blankets when you get him up there. Tie a towel tightly round where he's bleeding most—the wrist I think. Get him some warm *tea*. Keep him quiet until the doctor comes. Have you got that? And *you*—see if you can get his jacket cleaned up." She thought. "You'd better phone his home and tell them he's on his way, so they can get ready for him. Oh yes, and get a bottle of brandy. He may need it when the doctor's finished with that dog bite. The *best* brandy."

The young men, next to each other, nodded solemnly in unison, and Mel could feel another fit of giggles building up.

Mr St Clair moaned and swayed. Mel propped him up. "Now here's the lift. The manager will show you to a nice quiet room. And there's a doctor coming to see to your bite. You'll soon be on your way home."

134

Mr St Clair clutched her hand. "You are a very kind girl. I am much indebted. When I am myself again . . ."

"That's all right," said Mel. "Don't worry about a thing."

"But I've forgotten your name."

"Mel Calder."

"Oh yes," he said. "I remember now. Mitch Hamilton's fiancée."

"That's not . . ." said Mel. But it was too late. The lift doors had closed.

She turned away, letting her laughter go, and bumped into a heavily-built man with a red face in a heavy check suit, who was standing listening.

He shook her hand. "You handled that very well. Order out of chaos. I didn't catch the name."

"Mel Calder."

"McKinley."

He obviously expected her to recognise it. A producer? A manager?

He looked at her closely. "I didn't know Mitch was getting married."

Nosey Parker. She couldn't be bothered to explain. "Didn't you?" she said, still laughing, and went back to the reception room, in time to see Roxy Leigh being carried out on a stretcher, moaning, her eyes closed, her hand with its long black talons holding her forehead delicately, accompanied by two press photographers. Mel had to hand it to her, she never missed a trick.

Mel picked her way through the debris. The sober and respectable guests had gone, leaving groups of laughing and mostly drunken musicians. In one corner the members of a well-known band were having a battle with the jelly trifles.

Mitch and Barney had been joined by three other young men. They were all sitting on the floor, their backs against the wall, legs stretched out in front, sheltered from the jelly fight by the bulk of the table. They were peacefully gnawing at chicken legs and passing a bottle of champagne from hand to hand.

Mel looked at them casually, and nearly let out a yelp. Night Mission! Her very favourite band. Ronnie, Mike and Cliff of Night Mission in person. Fantastic. Feeling shy she went over to them.

Mitch said, sourly, "You've finished holding St Clair's hand, then."

Mel went pink. "He's in shock."

"Yeah. A terrible thing. Vodka and coke all over his pretty suit."

"Not coke, blood," said Mel, mildly. "That's why I took him out. I thought you might want your contract renewed."

They all stopped eating to stare at her.

Barney patted the floor. "Come and sit down, love."

She looked at the food-encrusted carpet and decided against it. Better to risk a flying jelly. She picked a tablecloth off the floor, wiped the table clean and sat on it, relieved to be off the three-inch heels for a while. She ran her fingers through her hair. It felt incredibly soft and light. She found they were all looking at her.

"You never told me promotion parties were like this," she said to Mitch, to cover her embarrassment. "It looks like that disco place in the High Street after the last police raid. I suppose the presentation is off?"

"I tell you, it's the best promotion party I've ever been to," said Mike Adams, grinning. "It'll set a new fashion."

"It's all right for you," said Mitch morosely, "I'll never live it down. Never. And who's going to be on the carpet tomorrow?"

"A dozen cleaners I should think," said Mel, smiling. "I'm starving. Where did you get your food?"

"Help yourself," Mitch waved an expansive hand.

"The cat's been sniffing it all."

"It's a *clean* cat," said Cliff Hawkins, offended.

136

"It'll be a dead one, if you let it go on eating chicken bones," she said. "They splinter in the stomach."

"What?!"

Alarmed, Cliff began to crawl under the tables. "Sammy, Sammy, Sammy . . ."

Mel tried to restrain herself, but the hysteria of the whole situation got to her again, and she threw back her head laughing helplessly.

"He knew Roxy would bring the dog, so he brought Sammy," Mike explained. "He's got a score to settle with her."

"I don't think the cat was necessary. The place was falling apart already. But it's all right. I won't talk." She grinned.

They watched her curiously. "What's your name, love?"

"Mel Calder."

"I'm Mike Adams and this is Ronnie . . ."

"Craig. Yes, I know. Night Mission." She smiled at them shyly. "I'm a fan. I wear one of your badges."

Mike smiled back, looking her over. "You fancy a meal, love? We're going some place to eat soon."

"Listen," said Barney, indignantly, glancing at Mitch who seemed sunk in silent gloom. "Keep your eyes off. She's Mitch's girl. They're getting married."

Mel smiled at Mitch, waiting for him to deny it—explain it was all a joke. He glanced at her fleetingly and then away. Incredibly, he was silent.

"Hey, that's great," said Ronnie Craig, beaming and slapping Mitch on the back. "I thought Roxy had hooked you."

Mitch said, avoiding Mel's insistent gaze, "We've kept it a secret."

Mike laughed. "You had a narrow escape there. That Roxy!"

Ronnie said, "It's not a secret any more. Melvin McKinley was on the phone outside."

Mitch groaned. Mel said, "Who is this McKinley?" just as Cliff came back with his holdall turning itself into strange shapes. "I'll take Sammy home and see you later. Where'll you be?"

They all stood up and began arguing the rival merits of the San Andreas and the Explosion.

Mel turned to Mitch. She said quietly, "You are a *rat*. I knew there was something. Nobody pays out that kind of money for nothing. You could have told me. *Warned* me."

"You wouldn't have come," he said, bluntly. "Besides, you won't believe this, but I didn't plan it like it happened. I mean, I guess I just, er, panicked."

"Well, what am I going to do now? You'd better tell her quick that it was all a joke. Before she sticks a knife in me. You going to hire a bodyguard?"

He smiled suddenly and put his arm round her waist. "I'll guard your body for you, Mel."

She tried to push his arm away. "Now look, Mitch . . ."

"Honestly, I'll protect you from Roxy."

"You'll *protect* me?" She looked around the wrecked room and started to laugh again. "I thought it was going to be so plush and up-market."

Mitch looked tense. "Mel, you won't tell anybody the truth yet? Promise?"

"All right," she said, reluctantly. He was already embarrassed. She couldn't make it worse for him. "I won't say anything. But you'll have to do something about it quickly. Tell the papers or something."

He sighed with relief and drew her closer. "Has anyone ever told you that you're a real tasty chick?"

"Not recently—Mickey Sweetiebums."

His eyes gleamed. His grip tightened and he leaned forward and brushed his lips against hers. She tried to slide off the table away from him, but laughing, he kissed her again.

"Hey, you two, break it up," Barney said. "We're all going along to the San Andreas."

Mel said shakily, "I don't think . . ."

"The desk?" Mitch said, quickly. "Don't forget the desk."

Mel sighed.

Barney, Mike and Ronnie were already on their way to the door. Impatiently Mitch scooped Mel off the table and hurried her, protesting, after them. His mood seemed to have changed suddenly. His eyes were shining and brilliant, laughing into hers. Mel looked away. He was really very attractive. She could see now why all the girls in the fan club at school fancied him. If it wasn't for the way she felt about Keith she might be in real danger.

The San Andreas was a club for professional musicians —small, relaxed, and not too crowded. It had good food and a live band and it was very expensive. They sat together at a big corner table and ate a huge meal.

Mel looked round the table. She could hardly believe it. She held back the giggles. "You *shall* go to the ball, Cinders!" Every girl's dream. They wouldn't believe her at school if she told them that she was in a club with three members of her very favourite band, Night Mission, and two members of the band currently number one in the charts, dressed up and being stared at, discreetly, by all the people at the surrounding tables.

Somewhere along the way, Mike and Barney had found two more girls. Mel was hazy about where they had come from, but they seemed very nice. Everybody was in an hilarious mood. Every so often someone would remember something else that had happened at the presentation and they would all explode with laughter again. Mike said he had managed to get hold of Roxy's wig and was going to give it to Cliff as a trophy.

139

Mel was getting a pleasant floating feeling from the wine served with the food. There was lots of wine.

"Who's paying for all this?" she said into Mitch's ear, at last, worried.

He looked amused. "It's just a meal. Don't worry—you won't have to do the washing up!" He slid his arm around her and kissed her neck.

Maybe there was too much wine. Mitch seemed to be getting into a very romantic mood. She eased his arm away, but in a few minutes it was back, and he was kissing her ear very gently. She knew she ought to do something to stop him, but she felt so warm and secure and comfortable, she couldn't be bothered. She knew it didn't mean anything special. It was just the way rock musicians were.

She danced with Cliff, with Mike, with Barney, and most of all with Mitch, who made her dance all the slow dances with him, holding her against him very closely. She began to feel hot and rather strange. Her lips and body felt strange too. Sensitive, tingling. She drank some more wine to steady herself, trying not to let Mitch see her hands shaking.

Later on they left the club and went back to someone's flat to listen to some fantastic old blues records and drink more wine. There were soft deep carpets and soft deep sofas, and then there was only Mitch, by himself, kissing her wildly, touching her. She found she was kissing him back.

Sixteen

Mel stared at the moonlight reflections on the ceiling over Mitch's bare shoulder. The patterns shifted as the wind moved in the tall trees in the street outside.

All that fuss about nothing, she was thinking, amused, disappointed. The Great Mystery. Hardly anything. It hadn't even hurt. It was all wrong what they told you. She had not intended to go so far, but one thing had led to another and then there seemed no good reason to stop.

He had been still a long time now. Had he gone to sleep? She moved a little, experimentally. At once his arms tightened possessively around her and he began to stroke her again, his hands gentle and loving, but greedy too. About twenty minutes, Mrs Bell had said, but they all thought she meant *once.*

She was surprised Mitch was like this. He had seemed too wound-up and intense to be so sexy. Not at all like some of the boys at school who were always on about it. Was he always like this, or was it just the extra excitement, the wine maybe, or the mad reception?

She wondered suddenly what had happened to all the other people at the club. Barney . . . Mike . . . Were they all doing this? Funny how everybody seemed to like it so much. She thought of all the people all over the world doing it all the time and had to stop herself laughing aloud. It was really crazy. Even Keith Edwards might be doing it.

She thought of his nice curling crisp hair, his wide

shoulders, the way his shirt was always coming out of his jeans when he bent over the desk, the glimpse of brown skin. She wondered what it would be like to be lying here with him, being touched in this new place, *his* body against her. Suddenly, without warning, her body lifted and exploded into feeling. She clung to Mitch gasping. She heard him saying, "Oh Christ, Mel" before all the words were swept away in a flood of sensation.

The moonlight had been replaced by grey morning light when Mel woke again. She rolled away from Mitch's arms, and went to find the bathroom.

It was luxurious. *Warm*. Shades of brown with thick creamy towels. The bath was sunken, with gold taps. There were fitted walnut cupboards and mirrors. How marvellous to own a bathroom like this. How marvellous to be able to *design* a bathroom like this. Mel wandered around, impressed and admiring.

She felt good. Wide awake. It was when she experimentally opened the shallow cabinet over the washbasin that it all turned sour. A medical cabinet. Prominent on the first shelf was a packet of Durex.

Condoms. Contraceptives. The bottom dropped out of her stomach. She felt faint. *Why on earth hadn't she remembered?* She must have been out of her mind.

She sat down on the dressing stool and put her head in her hands, her heart beginning to pound unpleasantly. She tried to think, but her panic was too great. All she could remember was Mrs Bell in the Human Biology lessons: "Having unprotected sex is just about the most *stupid*, irresponsible thing anybody can do." Mel had agreed, sure it would never happen to *her*. She groaned. It must have been the drink. Her father, a Scot, had had a saying about that. "Drink in, sense out." He was right. She hadn't *thought*.

But why hadn't Mitch, when he had the things handy?

There was a light layer of cold perspiration all over her skin. She felt the sudden need to wash herself all over. She turned on the shower hastily. It wouldn't make any difference, but it might make her feel better.

"Where have you been?" Mitch leaned up on one elbow. He was smiling, his hair falling over his forehead attractively. "I've been waiting for you."

Mel looked away. "Having a shower."

"A *shower*!"

"People do."

"Not in the middle of the night."

"It's nearly eight o'clock."

"The middle of the night!"

She stood at the end of the bed and put her hands across her, pretending to rub her arms, embarrassed at the way he was looking all over her.

"You'll catch cold. Come back to bed." He pulled back the cover and she looked away hastily, the colour rushing up her cheeks. She tried not to think of last night, but just the sight of his body had started that strange kind of trembling again.

"Where are we? What is this place?"

"Where d'you think? It's my flat, of course."

"*Your* flat?" She began looking for her clothes quickly. "I've got to go to school. I'll be late."

He sat up abruptly. "You are joking?"

"Of course I'm not. There's a special group going to look at the William Morris stuff in the V & A. I've got to go to school!"

He lay back and put his arms behind his head, watching her. "I thought you'd stay with me. Have the day off."

"Can I get the Underground near here? Where are we?"

"Mel . . . ?"

"*No!*" She wasn't going to lose control again.

143

"I'll drive you to school afterwards."

She found her bra on the floor by the bed and began to put it on, her hands shaking. "I can't go to school in a silk suit and high heels."

"Home and then school."

"No . . ."

"*Yes!*" He leaned forward swiftly, put one arm around her knees and tugged her off balance. She fell against him and he held her close, laughing, feeling her trembling. "You really want to."

"You'll make me pregnant."

He tightened his arms around her. Unexpectedly he was laughing again. "Great! We're engaged aren't we? What are you worrying about?"

But already Mel had managed to wriggle away and was dragging on the rest of her clothes.

"I said *No*, Mitch, and I mean it."

Mitch drove her home grumbling all the way. She dashed in, changed into her school uniform and flat shoes, grabbed her school bag and ran back to the car. Thank God everybody was out. Mrs Miller would want to know where she had been all night and she had no idea what she was going to say.

She made Mitch stop two streets away from the school. She did not want any awkward questions from friends about what she was doing getting out of a white Mercedes driven by Mitch Hamilton of Assassination and being kissed by him too.

She pulled her mouth away, breathless. He said, laughing, "What about the desk?"

She had forgotten the desk.

"I'll bring it round. Got a key?" She gave him her second door key and rushed off.

The school bell had gone twenty minutes ago. School was in Assembly. She ducked past the hall and the cloakroom and made it up the stairs to the art room, without meeting anyone. As she had hoped, Mrs Bell was unlocking the stockroom.

"Mrs Bell, please, have you got a minute?"

She looked at Mel's white face and dark, panicking eyes. "Come in the office. What is it?"

"How soon can you tell if you're pregnant?"

Mrs Bell groaned. "Oh, Jesus, Mel, don't tell me . . . After everything I said, after all those lessons, you went ahead without taking precautions?"

"It was different. You know, I didn't think about it once. And then I couldn't stop. I didn't *care*. I didn't realise it kind of took over like that." Mel's cheeks were scarlet. "And you said twenty minutes," she said, accusingly. "You never said more than once."

Mrs Bell groaned again. "I told you . . . Oh well, what's the point now? You'll have to get a test. Your doctor."

"No. Isn't there another way?"

"A lot of chemists do a pregnancy test. That big one in the High Street probably. You take in a urine sample. Or you could go up to the Brook Advisory Centre in Tottenham Court Road, number 233, I think it is. They help a lot of young people with problems. When was your last period?"

"I'm due this week. Today or tomorrow. I'm pretty regular."

"And when . . . ?"

Mel went even pinker. "Last night."

Mrs Bell blew out a relieved breath. "For Pete's sake, Mel, didn't you listen to anything in the Human Biology lessons?"

"Yes, but it didn't . . . well, it didn't sort of seem to be about *me*."

Mrs Bell snorted, exasperated. "The most dangerous time for getting pregnant is the second week after your period. Fourteen days from the first period day. You are most fertile in the *middle* of your cycle, *between* periods. Have you got *that?*"

"Yes," said Mel, ashamed, "I remember now. I just panicked."

"The first few days after your period, or the last few days before your period are not quite so dangerous—*if* you have a regular cycle, that is. The trouble is most people your age aren't regular—so it's *always* dangerous. Not to mention AIDS. You should never, absolutely *never*, have sex without taking precautions, however unromantic that sounds. In this case you may have been lucky. We have to hope so."

A thin line of sweat broke out along Mel's forehead and she sat down abruptly and put her head between her knees. Mrs Bell put her hand on Mel's shoulder. She said, severely, "You are a fool, Mel Calder. With all your other troubles."

"I know," Mel's voice was muffled. "I thought I could look after myself, but you know, I couldn't stop. It just took over."

"If it's like that . . . Have you got a piece of paper?" Mel looked up, dazed. She pulled her sketch book out of her shoulder bag and handed it over. Mrs Bell wrote an address in her large clear writing and gave it back.

"Get down there quickly—now—*today*."

"I can't. I'm going to the V & A."

"Ring up when you get back and explain to them. No later. They'll give you a test. They can give you a morning-after pill to bring on your period early, if they think it's necessary. And they'll set you up with protection. The Pill maybe."

"But I won't ever . . ."

Mrs Bell exploded. "It's not something you turn on and off like a tap. Surely you've learned that already? Next time you may not be so lucky. And what about your boyfriend?"

Mel, red, said, "I haven't got a . . ."

"Does he know you've decided to give it up?"

"But I won't . . ."

"But you *did*, Mel. You told me. Suppose it just 'takes over' again?" She sounded sarcastic.

Mel looked at her dumbly.

"Promise you'll go. What kind of life could *you* give a poor bloody unwanted baby?"

Mel stared at the floor, shaken and upset. "Yes, I suppose I'd better. Yes, I will. Thanks a lot, Mrs Bell."

"You're all right, Mel. Responsible. Not like some. Don't worry. They'll be very helpful. It won't hurt and it's not embarrassing in any way. Just don't forget, or put it off, that's all. The museum group are in the car park by the way."

"I'd better go down then. They'll go without me."

"Are you all right?"

"Yes, I feel better. Thanks a lot, Mrs Bell."

Clutching the sketch book she reached the door just as it opened suddenly and Keith Edwards strode in. The book flew out of her hand and landed at his feet.

Keith said, "Sorry, Mel," and picked it up. He glanced at it casually and read upside down, in Mrs Bell's large printing: FAMILY PLANNING CLINIC.

Incredulous, his eyes reached Mrs Bell. She frowned a warning at him. Mel snatched the book back under her arm.

Keith said, "Okay, Mel, I've just got some things to pick up. I'll be down in a second and we'll be off. The bus is at the front gate. The others are there already." Mel went out thankfully.

Keith said, angrily, "What's this all about then?"

"It's nothing to do with you, Keith. Mind your own business. But go easy with her today. She's upset."

He was annoyed and jealous. "She is my business. I'm her Group Tutor."

"Then she'll probably tell you."

147

"Christ Almighty—she's not pregnant? Mrs Green will boil my liver."

"Mel got into a heavy scene and I gave her the address of the local Family Planning Clinic. She hasn't got a mother to advise her. That's *all*. Are you satisfied?"

"Why did she come to you, instead of me?"

"I suppose because I'm a woman and I do sex education with the Sixth, in case you've forgotten."

"I can't believe it. *Mel* of all people. I didn't know she was like that. I wonder who . . . When I find out who's screwing her I'll kill him."

Mrs Bell raised her eyebrows sarcastically. "Big Man talk. You're over-reacting a bit, aren't you? She's seventeen. It's not illegal. She's grown up suddenly this term. She's a lovely mature girl. Or hadn't you noticed? Not like you, Keith, sweetie."

Their eyes met and Keith Edwards' face flushed darkly. He stalked out, slamming the door.

Mrs Bell sat down at the bench and pulled a set of exercise books towards her. She stared down at them, and wondered if Keith Edwards realised the razor's edge he was walking with some of the older girls in the school. One slip, and he was going to be in very severe trouble.

Seventeen

Late in the afternoon Keith Edwards pulled the school minibus to the kerb outside Mel's front door. She was the last to be dropped off. He got out and unlocked the back door of the bus. She jumped down and dumped her school bag on the pavement.

Keith was looking along the road, surprised. "This road is looking up. I see the shop at the end is painted now. It's much better than when I was here last."

"Well you haven't been round for a good while." He had never explained about Christmas, either, and she still felt hurt when she remembered.

"We had a campaign to get rid of the rubbish and the dumped cars. But they ought to plant trees and flowers at the end there. Look, I've started to do the passage and stairs."

She opened the door with her key and he stood just inside, looking at the stripped walls. The wooden panelling half way up the walls had been rubbed down ready for painting.

Keith looked around, impressed. "You know, you've worked wonders here. And you've got a flair for colour too." He said suddenly, "Why don't you think about a College course, instead of looking for a job when you leave school. Interior Design, for instance, or Town Planning or even Architecture. You've still got time to get in an application if you hurry."

"Do you think I'd be good enough?" She went pink.

"I don't see why not. You've got a feeling for buildings,

149

colour, shape. You take a lot of care and you're willing to do all the hard unglamorous jobs as well. Think about it."

"I never thought of interior decorating." It was the first time any career had seemed remotely interesting. She had thought she would be lucky to get a job and almost certainly it was going to be dull and boring, and here was Keith suddenly opening a door of hope. "Yes, I'll think about it." A rainbow of excitement arched in her.

He watched her face, smiling. "You enjoyed the William Morris stuff today?"

"Oh yes," she said, fervently. "It was brilliant. Thank you for taking us." She smiled back at him, shining with happiness, her eyes dark and huge. He could not resist the impulse to make her react to him as a man, not as a teacher.

He said, low, "I liked it too—you being there." He looked into her eyes, tempting her.

Mel hesitated, then dazed, put her hand on his shoulder and stood on tiptoe to kiss his cheek. At the last minute he turned his head and her soft lips slid against his. He felt her immediate response. Hot for it, he thought. And she was already wasting herself on some spotty little teenager. He kicked the front door shut and kissed her again, not lightly, not gently. She put her arms around his neck.

"Good afternoon."

Over Keith's shoulder, Mel's eyes widened in horror. Mitch was leaning against the kitchen door, his eyes bright, fierce, sardonic.

Keith spun round and they stared at each other.

Mel said quickly, her voice husky, "How did *you* get in?"

"Delivering the desk. You gave me the key, remember?"

The desk. She had forgotten their arrangement. Almost forgotten what had happened last night in the excitement of being with Keith all day, looking at beautiful things with him. She had not thought about Mitch once. She said, stammering, "K-Keith, this is a friend. His grandad owns

150

the junk shop where I work. I've just got this fantastic desk . . ."

Mitch interrupted rudely, "Who's *he*?"

"My art teacher. He, er, kind of keeps an eye on me."

"His hands too, by the look of it."

Mel went scarlet.

Keith was worried. How much had the guy seen? He said, bullying, "I'm Keith Edwards, Mel's Group Tutor."

Mitch laughed and parodied his pompous manner. "And I'm Mitch Hamilton, Lead Guitarist with Assassination. Mel's *lover*."

Keith looked at her, shaken.

"It's not true," cried Mel, horrified.

Mitch let his eyes swing over her reminiscently. "I don't know what we were doing in my bed all last night and this morning, then."

Mel wished the floor would open up. An impossible nightmare.

Keith said, "You should have told me, Mel. I would have understood. You've been taking terrible risks."

"Keith, I swear it's not true. I'm not his . . . lover. It wasn't like that."

"She's a real loving lady," drawled Mitch, taunting. "Too bad you have to miss it, *Dad*."

Keith turned his shoulder and spoke directly to Mel. "Were you with him last night?"

He read the answer in her scarlet face and averted eyes. "Mel, you've got to think about what you're doing. You can't throw everything away just when it's all starting for you. You've had a bad time, and I can understand the temptation. A good-looking bloke like that. A pop star at the top of the charts. Glamour. Fame. Money. A car. All the trappings. But you know there's nothing in it, don't you? No future. No security. No lasting relationship. He'll love you and he'll leave you."

151

"What do you know about it?" Mitch said, furious.

"Of course I know that!" Mel said impatiently to Keith. "You don't have to tell me. I can work it out for myself."

"I can't stop you, Mel, but you're at risk, and I think I'll have to have a word with Dee Tracey."

"It's nothing to do with Dee Tracey!"

Mitch said, urgently, "Mel, I've got to talk to you. Look . . ."

But Mel could not bring herself to look at either of them. She felt she was living a nightmare. She swallowed. "Keith, please, you don't understand."

"I'm leaving now, but you've got to promise me you won't go with him again until you've done some serious thinking."

"All *right*," Mel said, "but if you'd only listen . . ."

Keith looked at Mitch coldly. "I think you'd better come with me."

"No thanks, *Dad*, I like it here." He smiled derisively. "I don't need a lift. My car's outside. The big Mercedes."

Keith was suddenly conscious of his old cords and crumpled shirt. He looked at Mitch's expensive leather jacket and sour envy flooded over him. It would be a pleasure to punch his head in.

Mitch watched him. He said, softly, "Don't try it."

"Keith, please listen, he isn't . . ."

He had turned and flung open the door.

"Keith!"

"I'll see you at school Mel and we'll talk. But be careful and use that address Mrs Bell gave you as soon as possible. Look, don't come in tomorrow morning. Go there instead. D'you hear?"

"Yes, yes, *all right*, but Keith . . ."

But he had gone, slamming the door behind him. She heard the gears of the old bus grinding off. She leaned her forehead against the door.

Mitch stood watching her. "You go round kissing all your teachers like that?"

She turned angrily, her cheeks wet, and brushed the tears away with the back of her hand. "How could you, Mitch? It's the first time he's kissed me, really noticed me, then you go and ruin everything. I thought we were friends. I'll never forgive you, telling lies like that."

"What lies?"

"You know. Making him think I was your girl. It's not true—you know it's not. He's gone away thinking it's a big thing between us and all it was . . ."

He said, still and tense, "Yes, what was it, Mel?"

She looked at him bitterly. "You ought to know. You're the one with all the experience. It was just casual. What do they call it—a one-night stand."

"That all?"

"I had too much wine, and I suppose you were lonely or something. I was available and you just used me."

He gave a vulgar crack of laughter. "You were available all right. *Eager* would be a better word."

Mel said, huskily, trying not to burst into tears, "I suppose you thought you'd paid for it and might as well have it."

Mitch went white with anger, but she did not notice.

"I must have been crazy," Mel went on. "And now he thinks we're together and he won't ever kiss me again, and he'll go back to that snooty bitch I saw him with."

"So what?"

"So I can't bear it!" Her voice rose.

"You're in love with him."

"What's it to you?"

"I'm just trying to figure out why you were so loving to *me* last night." His eyes narrowed. He moved forward swiftly and tilted her head, roughly, so that he could look in her eyes. "You weren't by any chance pretending I was *him*?"

Mel pulled away, scarlet, but he had already dropped his

153

hands away, and stood hunched, looking at her with dark, contemptuous eyes.

"That's disgusting."

Mel said, desperately, "I couldn't help it. And not all the time anyway. What does it matter? It was just one night. It's all done with."

He laughed grimly and tossed her an evening paper.

"Sorry, *sweetheart*. Not yet. We're engaged, remember?"

There was a large picture of Mitch, looking moody and exciting, under a heading, *Mitch Hamilton to Wed*, with the reporter's by-line, *Melvin McKinley*.

Mel looked up, stunned, "But Keith will see this," she stammered. "*Mrs Miller*. My mother! They'll *all* see it. Oh, Mitch, what on earth can we do? You'll have to get on to the paper straight away, *now*, and tell them it's a terrible mistake."

Mitch looked at her for a long moment, then, silent, walked past her out of the house.

The news that Mel Calder was going to marry Mitch Hamilton of Assassination created a sensation throughout the school the next morning. Somehow Mel lived through the teasing, the snide remarks and the dirty jokes, trying to seem cool, but wincing inside. She learned to turn aside rude questions.

"It's all a mistake," she said, over and over again. "It's all lies."

They were disappointed. "You mean you ain't getting married, Mel?"

"Of course not. It's just newspaper talk."

She even lived through the embarrassing interview with Keith Edwards and Dee Tracey.

She didn't try to make up a story for Mrs Miller. She simply explained what had happened. When she had finished, she waited apprehensively for the axe to fall, but

154

Mrs Miller said quietly, "Lucinda said you would be late from the presentation, and might have to stay over with Mitch. Next time I want to hear about it from you. Do I deserve to be worried out of my mind?"

"I'm sorry," said Mel, ashamed, knowing there was no possible excuse. "I won't do it again."

"You need a lot of loving, I know, Mel. You've not had your fair share. But don't go looking for it in the wrong way." Then she put on her coat and took Mel directly to the Family Planning Clinic.

Mel waited for Mitch's denial to appear. Every day she looked through all the newspapers in the library, but there was nothing. Mitch did not come to the shop and an uncanny silence seemed to have settled over Assassination.

"I've not seen him," said Lou, holding court in his favourite corner of the hospital day room. "He'll be on the road, I reckon."

"Please Lou, ask him to call round when you see him next. I've got to talk to him about . . . s-something important."

"I saw the paper," said Lou. "Getting your bottom drawer together then?"

"No!" said Mel, angrily. "And it's *not funny*. Just tell him I want to see him urgently."

To her annoyance Mel found that suddenly she was very popular with the boys. The prestige of taking out a girl who was a friend of Mitch Hamilton was very high. Before, they had hardly noticed her, now she was showered with invitations to parties, discos, clubs, and recognised by everyone at school, even the staff, who usually said, "Mel who?"

"It's stupid," she said to Lucinda and Ben, sitting at the evening meal. "Nobody wanted to know me before, when I needed friends and help."

"It's not their fault," said Ben. "You didn't join in. You

155

kept yourself to yourself in the background, like a little mouse. And let's face it, man, you weren't interested."

Mel laughed ruefully. "That's all you know."

Lucinda said, disgusted, "Boys are so *stupid*."

"Well, she's different now. She even looks different," Ben protested.

"My hair."

"No. More like a person . . . more real . . ." He struggled to make it clear and gave up. "I might even take you out myself."

"Robbed a bank?" drawled Lucinda, nastily. "You must have all of three pounds in your money box, sonny."

"Well, thanks for the thought," Mel grinned. "I realise what an honour that would be, but honestly, I don't think I'm ready for it yet, Ben. I'm not into younger men."

Eighteen

Mel sat at her desk with the late afternoon sun from the front window falling across its satiny surface. Homework was certainly less painful since she had acquired the desk.

She cut out and mounted the wallpaper samples she had got for the hall and staircase and studied them carefully. The walls had to be light because the hall was so dark and narrow. The woodwork would be white, of course, but should she choose the blue forget-me-nots, or the tiny scattered yellow daisies? She was hoping she could find a new piece of carpet in the market at a really low price for the entrance. If only she could afford to carpet the stairs as well. Luxury. So quiet the neighbours wouldn't hear you going to bed. She sighed. You couldn't hope for everything. The wallpaper ought to match the carpet.

Blue or gold? Gold maybe, because of the yellow in the back room. All the books said it was good to keep a colour theme going in a small house. And gold was more cheerful.

She slotted the new page into her loose-leaf project book next to the photograph of the hall in its original state, the measured ground plan, and the two watercolour paintings of alternative ideas for redecorating it. The project book was getting quite thick and impressive. Keith had said she should take it with her when she went to the interview for the interior decorating course. She had filled in the application forms and sent them off, but the grant position was unclear and with her mother away everything seemed so uncertain and probably hopeless. They might even make her get a job to support herself.

When she got depressed it was nice to look back at the original photographs and see the awful state the house had been in. But there was still lots to be done. The soft cover for the sofa, for instance, now draped invitingly over its back. Mel grinned. Her project to make a loose cover for the splitting sofa had filled the textiles teacher, Mrs Timms, with alarm.

"But Mel, it's much too difficult for you! These covers have to fit properly. Every part of the sofa has to be measured exactly." She stared at Mel's sketch. "There are these ears, and the way the legs stick out . . ."

"I want to cover them up with a pleated frill, like this." Mel produced a picture she had torn surreptitiously from a magazine in the school library. "I could saw the ears off," she offered.

"*Mutilate* it?" squeaked Mrs Timms, outraged.

Mel grinned. "It's been severely tortured already, Mrs Timms. Look, I've made a table, put up shelves and helped build a kitchen cupboard. I've learned to do wallpapering and get rust off an iron fireplace and sanded a whole floor. It can't be more difficult than that!"

"Well, I don't know," said Mrs Timms, doubtfully. "I suppose as you're so keen you could try it."

It was more difficult than Mel thought. It had to be unpicked three times before it fitted properly, but now she had only to hem the frill. *Only? Twelve metres?* Mel groaned. Why were things always so much more trouble than you thought? It would have to wait until after homework anyway. Sighing, she took out her English Literature. Her Mocks had been okay, but she felt she could do much better. *Had* to do better if she wanted to get a place at a college.

As she opened the set book there was a knock on the front

door. Mel glanced curiously out of the front window. Parked against the kerb was a glossy black Porsche.

Mel gaped at it. There was a second knock before she could reach the front door.

"Melody Calder?"

"Yes, that's me."

"I'm Polly."

She was a thin, laughing woman, quick-moving, beautifully dressed in a tan designer suit. She ran her fingers through her dark curly hair and sighed with relief. "There was so much traffic in Whitehall I was afraid I wasn't going to get here after all. And now I can only stay half-an-hour."

She seized both Mel's hands, holding them tightly. "Oh, I'm so glad to meet you, Mel. I thought you might be out. May we go inside?"

Mel managed to close her mouth and show her visitor into the front room.

"I had business in the Foreign Office and I simply couldn't get away. We have to fly back to the States this evening. I'm meeting my husband at Heathrow—he's flying from Geneva, and we have to be back at the UN tomorrow. I thought, I shall die of disappointment if I don't get to see her after all the conniving!"

"I'm sorry, I don't understand," Mel said, breathing in. "I didn't catch the name . . ."

"Oh my dear, what a fool I am. Mary Hamilton, Michael's mother."

Enlightenment exploded in Mel's head. Michael? *Mitch*. Mitch's *mother*. They looked very alike—the dark hair, the dark blue brilliant eyes. A horrible suspicion gripped her. Surely she couldn't have seen the newspaper reports? Surely she didn't know about the . . .

"As soon as I heard about the engagement I decided I must come over to meet my future daughter-in-law."

159

Mel closed her eyes. Another nightmare. "Mrs Hamilton . . ."

"Call me Polly. Everybody does. Let me look at you properly."

She held Mel's hands wide, and looked her over frankly. Mel was miserably conscious of her washed-out school blouse and old skirt, but she met the shrewd eyes directly.

"You are surprised."

"Staggered," admitted Mel. "I didn't know anything about Mitch's parents. I kind of got the idea he was an orphan."

Polly said, grimacing, "He's ashamed of us. We don't go with pop music. Too upmarket and stuffy. He can't stand our life style. Let me look at you again. I just can't believe it."

She went on staring. Mel, embarrassed and uncomfortable, said politely, "Would you like a cup of tea?"

To Mel's surprise Polly laughed. But the laugh broke in the middle and Polly pulled her close to hug her.

"Oh Mel! I can't tell you how relieved I am. All the way over I've been imagining terrible things. That you'd be one of these hard-rocking female singers with cerise hair. Or one of those intimidatingly beautiful model girls, so *superior*, or some horrible gold-digging little scrubber Mitch had got into trouble."

Mel went red. "Mrs Hamilton . . ."

"Oh you're blushing, you little love. I've not seen a girl blushing in years. I didn't think they did these days!"

"All the time," said Mel, ruefully, and could not help laughing.

"That's better. There's no need to be nervous. I haven't descended on you like a lioness to protect my darling son."

She took off her jacket, dropped it over the back of a chair and sat down smiling. "He's quite capable of looking after himself. I don't know why I've been worried. I ought to have known he would land on his feet. Just like a cat with nine lives.

"It's his father. He gets so upset. I'll admit that when we first heard the news we were worried. Mitch is young and his life is so unsettled and irresponsible. All that racketing about with Barney and the band. It drives my husband crazy. They quarrel all the time, my dear. He's always trying to make Mitch give up the band and settle down. But of course, it's hopeless. He just can't see it, and they fight all the time when they're together . . ."

Mel said hastily, "Mrs Hamilton . . ."

"Polly. I'll admit that I was hoping you might agree to wait a while before marrying, but I know you're going to say you are in love . . ."

"It's all *right*," said Mel. "I mean you don't have to worry . . ."

"Oh, I'm not worried at all now, my dear! That's what I'm saying. Now I've met you I think it's just the best thing Mitch could do. He's very intelligent, you know. A weird gene mixture, my son. Wild crazies on my side, and sensible, wise people on my husband's side. Mitch takes after me, I'm afraid, but sometimes, on the really important things, his father's family comes out. I always thought he might be very careful who he actually married. But you see he has been such a difficult, wild, boy."

Mel, annoyed, said coldly, "I suppose he had reasons."

"Well, of course, you're bound to be on his side, but he *has* been difficult. He was always a kind of angry boy. Lonely and not very sociable. His father was a little too strong and strict. And then, he didn't like our kind of life. We work for the United Nations, you see, and we were moving about all over the world. Never a settled home, and there weren't many young people, so we sent him home to boarding school, thinking it would be more fun and he'd make friends. But that was a disaster too." She sighed. "You know, he ran away from *three* places?"

Mel said quickly, "Look, I don't think this is any of my business . . ."

"My husband and I have always been very close. Very much in love. Mitch is our only child and he always felt left out—no matter what we did."

It was getting worse. Mel said, firmly, "Please don't go on telling me all these private family things."

"Well, you have a right to know, Mel. Mitch has been lonely all his life. There was nothing I could do about it and I can't tell you how happy I am, what a joy and *relief* it is to know that he's found someone of his own at last."

"Please listen, Polly!"

"And you'll be just right for him, I can tell. Perfect."

"You don't know that at all," said Mel, desperately. "We've only just met."

Polly looked at her directly and smiled slowly. She ran her fingers through her hair. "Oh yes. I've got very good at meeting people and making snap judgements. You are shrewd and practical. You listen. You are interested. You are involved in life. You won't bend when the bitter wind blows. And you have plenty of love to give, although you try to cover that up, I think." She smiled. "No wonder Mitch got you engaged so quickly. You're a lifetime girl."

Mel said hotly, "I'm not pregnant, if that's what you mean."

"Of course not. I'm being clumsy. You're so vulnerable, Mel. No second skin. Mitch will love taking care of you. He's always wanted people to take care of. Someone of his own. I'm very happy about this engagement, and I know his father will be too."

"I'm sorry," said Mel, wearily. "I've been trying to tell you for ages—it's all lies."

"*Lies!*"

"The papers, everything. I'm not engaged to Mitch. I'm only seventeen. It was a joke."

"Not a very amusing joke."

Mel looked away.

"It looks as though Mitch is going to be badly hurt." Polly sounded very upset.

"It was his joke, not mine," said Mel, harassed. "Well, not a joke, exactly. A mistake."

"How can you possibly get engaged by *mistake*? If it's not true, why hasn't Mitch denied it to the media?"

Mel drew a deep breath, feeling how unfair it all was. How could she explain Roxy to Mitch's *mother*? She said, awkwardly, "Well, it kind of suited him not to say anything. There's a girl who's been a nuisance."

"Roxy Leigh. It's all right, you don't have to be so careful. We all know about Roxy Leigh."

Mel sighed with relief. "Well, then, you'll understand how it was. I went to this reception with Mitch and Roxy was there and Mitch said we were engaged on the spur of the moment, just to get her off his back. But a reporter called McKinley heard him, and the next thing it was printed in the papers that we were engaged. Mitch should have explained to you."

"But he did," said Polly, mystified. "I didn't hear of the engagement through the papers. Mitch told me himself. He rang me . . . oh, about two weeks before the papers had it. He said he was getting engaged. That's how I managed to arrange to come to Europe. I thought it might be ages before you could come to the States."

"Two weeks?"

They stared at each other, Polly puzzled and Mel disbelieving.

"He must have meant someone else," said Mel, at last, baffled. "Roxy, maybe."

"No, I remember it distinctly. I was so excited. He said

you were fierce and truthful and serious—that doesn't sound like Roxy does it? And," she smiled mischievously, "he also said you were very kissable."

A hot wave of colour flowed into Mel's cheeks. "It doesn't sound like me either!"

"But he told me all about you! About your mother being in hospital, and how you were redecorating the house all by yourself, and doing your A levels . . ."

Polly watched her anxiously. Mel felt hot all over. It was incredible. There must be a reason . . . He had planned it all. Suddenly, she thought she understood. He had *planned* to use her against Roxy. No spur of the moment panic. He had planned it from the beginning. That was why he had been willing to pay out so much cash for her to go to the party. And he had contacted his parents before, just in case the press rang them for confirmation. A slow rage began to build in her.

"You'll be late for the plane," she said.

"Oh heavens, yes, I will." Polly caught up her jacket. "I have to go, Mel. I can't understand what Mitch is doing. When I saw the papers knew about the engagement I telephoned him. We really do care about him, you know. He didn't say it was a mistake or a joke. He sounded excited and happy. Head over heels, in fact."

"Don't worry," said Mel, grimly. "I'll sort it out with him."

Polly hesitated, worried. "I don't know what to do. If only I didn't need to catch this stupid plane. I'm distracted. Mel, you will think carefully, won't you? Please write to me and let me know . . ."

She sorted through her bag and gave Mel a card. "Oh, I'm so disappointed I could cry. I'd really love you for a daughter. Oh well!" Dabbing her eyes, she hugged Mel and made for the door.

"Write to me."

Nineteen

Mitch was on tour in Europe. He had sent a picture postcard of the Leaning Tower of Pisa, followed by a five-page letter with sketches, suggesting a plan for turning the back yard into a paved patio with potted plants, Italian style. He enclosed a cheque and suggested Mel should order the concrete and paving stones at once so that he could start the job as soon as he got home. There was no mention at all of the phoney engagement.

Angrily Mel tore up the cheque and threw the letter into the rubbish bin.

Mitch came back with Barney two weeks later. They tramped into Number Six, looking tired and very pleased with themselves.

"Sit down. Make yourself at home," she said, sardonically, watching Barney stretching himself luxuriously on her new pink sofa cover.

"Great to be back. Home," he said, grinning.

"Good trip?"

"Great, really great." Mitch sat down next to Barney and stretched out his legs. "Italy's great. They really appreciated us."

"That's good," said Mel, sourly.

"What wouldn't I give for a cup of real tea."

"I'll make it." Mel went reluctantly into the kitchen.

Mitch followed her and put his arms round her. "Don't I get a kiss?"

"No!" But he kissed her all the same. She twisted away, shaken.

"Did you get my letter? I see you've finished wallpapering the staircase and hall. It looks good. Did you get the concrete and . . ."

She carried the tea into the front room. "I've been waiting to see you. I've had visitors."

Suddenly she was very angry, feeling the injustice. Why should she have to deal with all the problems? And what right had he to go round kissing her like that?

"Yeah?" He was wary, picking up the hostile vibrations.

"Your mother."

"What!" He shot off the sofa again, as though he had sat on a pin. At any other time Mel would have laughed, but now she was too angry.

"I didn't know she was in London, even. Why didn't she tell me?" He looked furious.

Mel said, grimly, "I never knew you had a mother, Mitch."

"What did she want? *Shut up*, Barney! What did she say?"

Barney had begun to laugh. "Everything. You can bet," he said.

"She made the trip to meet her future daughter-in-law," said Mel. "To say how *pleased* she was. That you'd phoned her and described me, and you seemed to be so *happy* and *head over heels* . . ." To her surprise a wave of colour flooded up his neck and over his face.

Barney hooted again. "There you are."

"Very funny, Barney," said Mel. "I wish I could laugh too. But it was awful. You are a *pig*, Mitch. You phoned your mother two weeks before that reception. You planned it all in advance to get Roxy off your back permanently. It didn't happen on the spur of the moment, like you made me think. You covered your tracks with your parents in case the press got to them, I suppose. It was a real dirty trick."

166

"Mel . . ."

"You never even thought how it would be for me, did you? You just disappeared, leaving me to explain to everybody, including your mother. She was so nice and so pleased. It was terrible. I felt really rotten."

"What exactly did you tell her?" Mitch was tense.

"The truth. About the reception and that it was a joke and then she was really upset. Thought it was *my* joke and told me off for hurting you. Honestly, Mitch, I could kill you. She kept telling me all this private family stuff and I couldn't stop her. It was one of the worst times in my whole life. She's so nice and she'd come all this way . . ."

Mitch went and looked out of the window, hunching his shoulders.

"You said visitors. Plural," Barney said.

"Oh yes, that's right. I was forgetting the other visitor. A friend of yours. *Roxy Leigh.*"

Mitch spun round, incredulous. "Roxy came *here*? But how . . . ?"

"In a big limo. Chauffeur. No dog, though. All these big cars—Nosey Flo must think I'm running some kind of kinky sex parlour."

"Leave the jokes, Mel. What happened?"

"We didn't sit drinking cups of tea in sisterhood, I can tell you. She said she was going to do me in, in a very, er, unlikely way."

Mel was enjoying herself now, watching his face. Mitch did not laugh. "And?"

"There was quite a lot of that. Mitch, you've got to get this phoney engagement cleared up quick. I can't stand any more visits from your wild women, begging me not to marry you. Throwing themselves at my feet. Sobbing. Threatening suicide."

They stared at her in horror.

"S-she didn't! Even Roxy wouldn't . . ."

"I know what it is," said Barney. "She's finally flipped her lid."

"It was like an old Hollywood movie," said Mel. "It's a good thing I'm used to mad people."

Mitch was furious. "This is incredible. She's just got to be stopped."

"How did you get rid of her?" Barney was interested.

Mel grinned. "I got right into the part. I was very noble and good. I agreed to Give Mitch Up. I said I hadn't understood and that for the Sake of his Future Career and Happiness, I would Renounce him Forever!" She smiled with satisfaction. "You seen Garbo in *Camille* on the box? Then Roxy sat and told me how she felt about you Mitch, and we cried on each other's shoulders, and I said I'd put in a word for her when I saw you again."

Mitch did not laugh. He was white and angry. Barney took one look at him and stopped laughing too. Mitch drew a long, slow breath. "Let's get this straight. You told Roxy you'd break our engagement and talk me into marrying *her*?"

"Well . . ."

"Thanks a lot, *friend*."

"Look, you promised to sort it all out. Then you slid off. You're manipulating me, Mitch, and I don't like it. I've had a lot of trouble. The people at school, Keith, Mrs Miller . . ."

"You went back on our deal."

"You can have the desk back. It's not worth another session with your ma."

"Sod the desk!"

"Language," said Barney, reprovingly.

"I won't be manipulated, Mitch. I was going to tell Roxy we'd never been engaged and it was all a mistake, but . . ."

Mitch stared at her for a long moment. She thought that he was going to slap her, and then she saw with alarm that his dark eyes were suspiciously bright. She said, hurriedly, "She's crazy about you, Mitch. She really is."

168

Mitch stuffed his hands into his jeans and swung away.

"Mitch couldn't introduce her to his mum and dad," said Barney, explaining. "I mean to say, I wouldn't introduce her to my mum in Peabody Buildings. Can you imagine Roxy at a UN cocktail party?"

Mel said, accusingly, "I think you're a snob, Mitch. And that's another thing. You never mentioned your parents."

Mitch said wearily, "They couldn't be bothered with me. I kept getting sent away to school. They only want each other."

"I thought you were one of us. The underdogs. You're a fraud, Mitch. You're *posh*."

He turned round, very angry. "Listen, can I help what my parents do, any more than you could help your mother's breakdown? I'm myself. You're trying to label me."

Mel shook her head slowly.

"What about my grandad, then? Is he *posh*? My father started half a mile from here and worked his way up the hard way."

"But your mum didn't," said Barney. "British Raj all the way. Polly wouldn't take to Roxy at all."

"You know, Mitch, I think you're really devious. The 'engagement', your posh parents, keeping quiet about being in Assassination. What else haven't you told me? I thought you went to school with Barney."

"So he did," said Barney, "after they chucked him out of his public school for smoking grass and dishing out CND leaflets. He stayed with his grandad and came to Thomas Conway with us. We gave him hell, but he made out all right. Then we got the band together. He's a great bloke, Mel. Honest!"

Barney went over and slapped Mitch on the shoulder. "Cheer up, man, it's not the end of the world."

"Leave off, Barney," Mitch said, morosely. "You've said enough."

169

"You've been trying to get it out for months. Now she knows. What's so terrible? She's not walked out, has she?"

"You don't understand a thing, Barney."

Mel was staring at the carpet. After all—what did it matter? She wasn't going to any UN cocktail parties either. Nothing had changed. She had never thought there could be anything permanent about their friendship anyway. All the same she wished she hadn't let herself be conned.

She shrugged. "Oh well. But I think you ought to give Roxy a chance, Mitch. She's quite nice under all that hype and drama. Maybe you could get her to change her style a bit."

Mitch had picked a large box of matches off the desk to light a cigarette, with a shaking hand. Now he smashed it down again, so hard that the box split and the matches sprayed over the carpet.

"Let's get this right. I don't *care* what my parents think of Roxy or any of my girls. I don't *care* about her either. I'm not in love with her and I'm not marrying her. And stay out of my business."

He turned on his heel and walked out, slamming the door so hard the windows rattled.

Mel stared after him, shaken. "He's really upset. I didn't think . . . He shouldn't have started all this engagement bit, Barney. I—it wasn't part of the bargain. It's made things s-so bad for me at school."

Barney picked at the new sofa cover, avoiding her eyes. "He thinks a lot of you, Mel."

"He said he would make an announcement, but that was weeks ago. He hasn't done anything."

"You know he's frightened of Roxy."

"I don't believe it. I think he's just stringing her along. It's not fair, Barney."

He blew out a long exasperated breath. "You've got it wrong, Mel. Honest."

"That's what she thinks too. If he doesn't want her, why doesn't he tell her the whole truth, straight out?"

Barney stared at her, riveted. "That's *right*, Mel. He ought to tell her the *whole* truth. That's the answer."

He got up and went out, leaving her wondering uneasily what new trouble he was stirring up.

Mel did not have to wonder long. At school the next morning, Mrs Bell put her copy of the *Mirror* on the desk in front of her, spread out at the centre page.

There was a big picture of Roxy doing her wolf-girl act, staring dangerously through wildly starched hair, at least two feet across, and wearing a tiny fur bikini top. Her hips were draped in an equally tiny bit of fur, revealing the length of her long legs.

> *Last night Roxy Leigh talked to the Mirror about her tragic love for Mitch Hamilton, lead guitarist and singer with Assassination, at Number Five this week with their single, Love Luck.*
>
> *"I'm trying hard to forget him. I was with him a long time. We went everywhere together. But now he's fallen in love with this other girl, Melody Calder. They are planning to get married in the summer."*

Mel drew a furious breath. *Barney.* She would kill him when she got her hands on him.

> *"I know I can't compete with Melody. She's much younger and prettier, with this fabulous figure. All I've got to offer is my love and my voice . . ."* (sob, thought Mel) *"I've always been so ugly."* (Mel groaned, angrily) *"When I understood how things were, I knew I couldn't stand in his way. I knew I must sacrifice my own love for his happiness. That's all I ever wanted—for him to be happy."*

Mel thought that if Roxy had not pinched her very own lines she would be crying in sympathy. She could imagine Roxy dabbing artistically at her mascara.

"I'll never love anyone like that again. I shall devote my life to my singing. I think you'll like my new album, Tearaway, which is coming out next week. We've got a thirty day tour of the UK lined up and then we are heading for Europe and the States and . . ."

Heartbroken, Mel thought. She skipped the next bit, which plugged the new album and the expected hit single, and read the last paragraph.

Last night, Mitch Hamilton was not available for comment, but Assassination drummer, Barney Black, confirmed that Mitch was engaged to mystery girl, Melody Calder. "He loves her very much," he said. "And his parents are real happy at the news."

Mel, breathing deeply, went on staring at the paper. She thought she would tear Barney's head off as soon as she saw him. Why was Roxy ready to finish with Mitch? Or did she actually believe Barney's lies? And what was Mitch himself thinking? Mel felt her face grow hot. She wondered suddenly if her mother saw the newspapers in the hospital. Mitch would *have* to issue a denial now.

Half an hour later, the art room door swung open, cracking back against the wall. Standing in the open doorway, one hand on hip, was Roxy Leigh, dressed from head to foot in skintight black leather.

How on earth had she got into school? Mel closed her eyes and prayed she would wake up.

"Melody, Baby! Why didn't you *tell* me? I can't let it

172

happen. You can't give him up!" Roxy swept across the art room, and flung her arms round Mel. "Baby, I came to tell you, I've made it all right for you."

Mel groaned. Scarlet, acutely conscious of the gaping art group around her, she said desperately, "How did you find me here?"

"A dear old lady called Florence in your road."

Mel groaned again. "Look Roxy, let's go outside."

"It's *Roxy Leigh*! Roxy!"

The form crowded round her, hardly believing.

"It really is."

"What you doing in this dump, Roxy?"

"Hey, Roxy your last record was brilliant. *Great.*"

"Roxy, oh Roxy can I please have your autograph . . ."

"Roxy, I've got all your records . . ."

Mel said, frantic, "Please, Roxy, let's get out of this madhouse. I've got to talk to you. That report—Barney is lying . . ."

But the form had closed around her. There was pandemonium in the room, and Roxy did not hear. She was too busy signing autographs.

"What's going on in here?" Keith Edwards' voice penetrated the din. He came hastily into the art room through the connecting door and stopped dead, staring at Roxy.

"Good grief! Rosie Leigh! It is you, isn't it?"

Roxy gave a shriek and flung her arms around him. "Keith! Keith Edwards! *Lover!*"

"You know each other," said Mel, dazed.

Keith was flushed and grinning. "We were at Art School together. Hey, Rosie, come and have a coffee in the staff room and tell me all the news."

In an uproar of boos, catcalls and whistles, Roxy was borne off, leaving Mel staring helplessly after her.

Later, just before the bell went for lunch, Mel saw them from the window, getting into Roxy's car and driving off.

Keith was laughing and he had his arm round Roxy's shoulders.

Roxy would eat him alive, thought Mel, gloomily, racked with jealousy. Roxy? *Rosie!* It was all Mitch's fault.

Twenty

"Look, I know you are moving now in the rarefied world of exotic pop stars . . ." said Lucinda, grinning. "Barney Black, Roxy Leigh . . ."

"Oh shut up," said Mel, irritably, coming down the ladder from hanging the new front curtains Saira's mother had made for her. "I have enough of that at school. What do you want?"

"To talk to you about bathrooms."

"Um, yes. Interesting," said Mel, sarcastically. "Bathrooms."

"Nice, clean, shining bathrooms, with chrome fittings and showers and inside loos."

"Yeah. I've heard of them. So what?"

"So what about a General Development Area, like the workman said?"

Mel backed away. "No, Lucinda. Absolutely *no*! I haven't got time. I've got to revise for my A Levels and I want to finish the house. My mother's been so much better since Easter they say they might let her out soon and . . ."

"Don't try to wriggle," said Lucinda. "Look, I've thought it all out. We'll hold a meeting in the billiard room upstairs at the George. Mrs Snow says she'll let us have it for free. Good trade—all the regulars, plus. We'll get the roads made into a General Development Area and get all the houses modernised and converted."

"You've had a brainstorm," said Mel. "We'll be dealing with the Council, remember? It's that litter campaign. All that power has gone to your head."

Lucinda smiled at her wolfishly. "You converted me, Mel, baby. You were the one who wanted to change things."

"I'm fed up with writing leaflets," said Mel, weakly, knowing she was losing the battle. "My mother could be home any time."

"No leaflets."

Mel looked at her suspiciously, and Lucinda burst out laughing. "We're going round to see people instead."

Mel groaned.

"Joe said it's better. Direct contact. He's going to help."

Mel looked at her beadily, but Lucinda seemed to be very interested in something outside the window. "By the way," she said, "Joe's not married. That house belonged to his dad, but he died."

"I get it," said Mel, wearily. "Why didn't you say straight out? All right. Never let it be said that I ruined a friend's love life . . ."

"How would you like a bath and an indoor lavatory, Mr Reynolds?"

"Listen, girl, I'd like a Cadillac and a holiday back home, but I can't afford them neither."

"How would you like new window frames and a lavatory inside, Mr Gupta?"

"Sorry, no money," said Mr Gupta, smiling and shutting the door smartly.

"How would you like your roof repaired and a bathroom, Mrs Christopolous?"

She sighed. "Don't have dreams, kyrie. It just makes living harder."

"Would you like to see the pavement repaired and trees

planted on the railway embankment, Mr Nicholls? To make the place look nice?"

"It used to be a nice neighbourhood once," said Mr Nicholls, heavily.

"Trees and flowers?" said Mel.

"Well no, not exactly. But you couldn't do anything with the place now. All the trees would get dug up."

They went home depressed. Mel felt as though her feet were dropping off and her throat was sore from trying to convince people. It was hard going, much harder than the litter campaign. Older people were so cynical and pessimistic. They really got you down sometimes. But they had some promises of attendance at the Public Meeting and Mrs Ranjit of Sylvan Street had said that not only would she attend the public meeting, but she would start to make another banner for when they marched on the Town Hall.

"Well, thanks," said Mel, uneasily. "But maybe we won't have to march to the Town Hall this time." We'll all be in gaol instead, she thought gloomily, remembering Lucinda's growing enthusiasm and militancy.

On Saturday Mel opened the shop as usual and was wrapping up a brass kettle for Mrs Ackroyd, one of the increasing band of regular customers, when Mitch slouched in moodily and threw himself on to a Victorian chaise longue. He had on an old tee shirt with an extremely rude picture on the front which Mel hoped Mrs Ackroyd wouldn't understand. His eyes were red-rimmed with smoke and fatigue and there were dark rings under them. Mrs Ackroyd's nose twitched. Had he been drinking too?

Mrs Ackroyd said, meaningfully, "If you like, dear, I'll wait while you serve this young man."

"It's all right," said Mel. "He's . . . er . . . the owner's grandson."

Mitch pulled back his lips and smiled at Mrs Ackroyd

widely and insolently. Her mouth compressed into a tight line.

"I'll come about the mirror another time, dear," she said, taking her parcel and marching out.

"She was a good customer," said Mel, regretfully. "What's the matter with you, then?"

"Nothing."

She shrugged and went into the back room to plug the kettle in. "You want coffee?"

"I suppose so."

"Don't force yourself," said Mel, exasperated.

He turned his back and looked out of the window. She put the coffee next to him.

"You look as though you could do with some sleep."

"I've been up all night in the studio, laying down the last of the tracks."

"Oh, good, the album's finished then?"

He grunted. "There's the mix."

"You're pleased with it?"

He shrugged and stared out of the window.

"If it's no good you can always do it again."

He snapped angrily, "It's fine. The best we've ever done. Why should it be no good?"

"I just thought . . . Look, why don't you go home and go to bed? You'll feel better when you've had some sleep."

"You're not my bloody mother."

"Sorry."

She went into the back and drank her own coffee standing by the sink, looking out over the yard. She had had the council van come and take away all the unsaleable mouldy rubbish. The yard was swept and clear now. She had planted some geraniums in tubs and painted the store room door a glistening black to match the shop front. She had thought that maybe they could expand into architectural and garden pieces. There were plenty of old houses locally being pulled down and modernised. Some of them had splendid flying dragons on the point of the roof, stone faces, plaster ceiling roses, decorative iron fireplaces . . .

But perhaps she ought to give the job up if Mitch was going to be so unpleasant all the time. Perhaps he didn't agree with what she was doing with the shop and wanted to get rid of her.

She turned and saw that he was leaning against the door frame, watching her, his eyes dark.

"Look, if I'm not doing this job right, and you want me to go you'd better say straight out."

"It's nothing to do with the shop."

Mel sighed. "What do you want then, Mitch? I thought we weren't speaking. You've not been round since you threw that temperament."

"Oh, you noticed." He was sarcastic.

"Of course I noticed. What do you take me for? I wanted to say I'm sorry. I didn't mean to upset you, Mitch. I keep thinking you're a friend like Lucinda and Ben and I can say what I like to you. But you're not. I forget that you're famous and a star and I've no right . . ."

She saw from his expression that she had said something wrong again. She sighed. "I don't know what I've said to upset you now. All I meant was, it's not my business what you do about Roxy. I don't know you well enough to be offering advice . . ."

It was getting worse. His eyes were bright and savage. He came and leaned against the sink next to her and she could feel the angry tension in his body, but his voice was deceptively soft.

"Funny, I thought we knew each other well." He let his eyes swing over her. "*Closely*."

Mel flushed and looked away.

"You can't get any closer than we've been."

"There's no need to keep reminding me!"

179

"Why not? You liked it a lot."

Mel went an even deeper red. She felt hot all over and her heart was banging unpleasantly against her ribs.

"You're in a really stinking mood again, aren't you? Why did you bother to come round?"

"How's Daddykins?"

"If you mean Keith, how should I know? I've been too busy."

"You mean you weren't with him last night?"

"No, of course I wasn't. I was out with Joe and Ben and Lucinda."

"I waited two-and-a-half hours."

"How did I know you were coming?"

"Who's Joe?"

"Joe Isaacs. He's an anarchist. We're running this campaign." She told him briefly about the plan to get the roads turned into a General Development Area.

He said, interested, "I'll come to the Public Meeting with you, if you like."

She stared at him. "But it's nothing to do with you. Why should you?"

"It's a good cause. I can support a good cause, can't I?"

"But if people know that *you're* there, we'll need the police. There'll be a riot. I thought you wanted to be anonymous."

He shrugged. "Okay. As you like."

"Look . . . I'm grateful, Mitch."

"Yeah," he said, ironically. "I can see. Pleased to see me too."

Mel was impatient. "As it happens, I am. I want to know when you're getting in touch with the papers about this phoney engagement? I've been looking every day, but there's still nothing. If you're busy, can't your manager handle it?"

"Roxy's still hanging around."

"But Roxy said she was giving you up. She came to school to tell me. Right into the art room. And then she went off with

180

Keith Edwards. They were at Art School together. Did you know her real name is Rosie?"

She began to wash her cup under the tap, running the water furiously. "*Rosie* Leigh!"

Mitch laughed and stood close behind her. He put his arms around her, sliding his hands up under her sweater. She tried to pull them away with wet slippery fingers, but he cuddled her closer and began to nuzzle her neck.

"I missed you so much, Mel."

"Let me go, Mitch."

"It seems a long time."

He kissed her ear, and she tried to twist away, knowing he could feel her body responding.

"Mel . . . ?"

"No!"

"Why not?"

"We're not in love and you're just using me. I don't want to get involved with you like that. It's a waste of time. I want something real and lasting."

"Your body likes me."

She was trembling, her knees weak, and she could feel his hands shaking too. How was it possible, she thought, wildly, that you could be in love with one person and yet another boy could have this effect on you?

"*Please*, Mel." His voice was thick.

The shop bell tinkled and Mel pushed him away. She went out and served a man who bought a silver brooch with 'Alice' engraved on it, then a woman who wanted a glass butter dish.

When she went back to Mitch he was sitting motionless on the old sofa, his hands hanging down between his knees, staring at the floor. Her heart bumped again. Was there something really serious? He looked desperate.

"What's the matter, Mitch?" She sat down next to him.

"We're going on the road again next month."

"Well, what's wrong with that? I thought you liked touring."

"It's okay."

"So?"

"So it's a world tour. We'll be away three months."

"That's fantastic. Oh, you are lucky, Mitch. All round the world. All those countries. Japan. Australia. The States . . ."

"*Three months.* I won't be around for three months."

"You'll have a marvellous time, seeing new places, getting new fans. I don't know why you're fed up. You're crazy. It's not up and down the motorway. If you're worried about Lou, I'll . . ."

"That's all it means to you," his voice cracked. "And what about you, Mel? What'll you be doing?"

She gaped at him. "Me? What do you think? I'll be taking my A Levels."

"And jumping into bed with that bastard as soon as he thinks it's safe. And I won't be around to do anything about it."

Mel leaped to her feet, an angry patch of colour on each cheek. "I take it you're talking about Keith. You're always making it dirty. Trying to muck it all up. Okay, I love him, but he's my teacher and he wouldn't dream of doing anything wrong. He *helps* me. I'd like you to go now, Mitch, and *don't come back.*"

"Don't worry. I won't."

Twenty-one

The Public Meeting was in full swing by the time Mel arrived late. Angry people were standing up and shouting all at once. There were about thirty people there, a much bigger turnout than they had estimated. Joe had elected himself Chairman, and was sitting back grinning.

"What we want is new roofs."

"Inside lavatories."

"Bathrooms."

"Pavement repairs."

"Damp courses."

"Hot water."

"New window frames."

"And trees on the railway embankment. Inside new iron railings. And daffodils so that we've got something nice to look at."

Joe hammered on the table with his beer mug. "Now then, Ladies and Gentlemen. We need a plan."

"Someone ought to go and see them buggers up the Town Hall."

"Someone who knows about houses. Knows what's to be done."

Everyone turned to look at Mr Miller. He said, wryly amused, "They won't listen to no Black man down there."

Mrs Atkins said, "They don't listen to nobody down there.

That's what we've got to do. Make 'em listen. Like in the litter campaign. We beat 'em then."

There was a murmur of agreement.

"Mr Miller is in the building trade. I vote Mr Miller is our representative."

"Hear, hear."

Mr Miller said, "There'll need to be more than one. We need a committee."

"Mr Nicholls," someone said. Everybody looked at the two men slyly and waited, breathless. They had lived next to each other for twelve years and, as far as anyone knew, they had never even said "Good morning" or acknowledged each other's existence.

After a second, Mr Nicholls looked unwillingly at Mr Miller and nodded his head stiffly. "Very well. I worked for local government until I retired. I might be able to assist on procedure." A slight smile disturbed his face like ice cracking under a winter sun. "I think we may be able to prepare a few little . . . er . . . surprises, to make 'em sit up and put their hands in their pockets."

At the end of the room Mr Singh put up his hand. "Perhaps I might be able to help too."

Everyone stared doubtfully at his gentle, serious face with its liquid dark eyes. "Behind the scenes only," he said apologetically, "I am no fisticuffs fighter. But I am a trained lawyer. Shortly I shall take my final examinations in English law. There will be a need for a legal adviser. But if you do not wish . . ."

"Mr Singh for the Committee?"

Everyone clapped.

"Joe Isaacs."

"Okay."

"Mel Calder."

"No," said Mel, firmly. "I've got A levels coming up and I've just heard my mother is coming home next week. Count me out for the committee. But I'll give a hand with the donkey work. What about Lucinda? All this was her idea. She ought to be Secretary."

Lucinda was voted in as Secretary. Joe winked at her and put his thumb up.

"Any more? Mrs Ranjit? Right, everyone. That's it. We've got our Development Association Committee. Here's to our success!"

The meeting broke up enthusiastically in a rush to get to the bar before last orders were called.

Outside, Lucinda was doubled over, laughing hysterically.

Mel said, "What's up now?"

"Can't you just see them—my big dad, and little Mr Nicholls, and pretty Mr Singh, stalking Councillor Wright down the Town Hall corridors? And Mrs Ranjit coming up behind with her banner? They don't know what's going to hit them at the Town Hall."

Twenty-two

Mel looked at the clock for the third time in ten minutes. It was nearly four. Surely her mother should have arrived by now? They had said she would have a minicab to bring her home so there was no need for Mel to meet her.

She went to the door again and stared up the street. At the end of the road a car hesitated, and went on past to Sylvan Street. Mel closed the door and went back through the house slowly, room by room, checking that everything was as perfect as it could be. She was shivering slightly with excitement, remembering all the problems, the solutions, the hard work.

She had not managed a gold carpet for the entrance hall and stairs, but she had unearthed an old green one for three pounds at the junk shop; it was almost the same shade as the front room carpet, and it had cleaned up well. Although there were joins in three places where she had had to cut away worn parts, they could hardly be seen and the carpet fitted neatly wall to wall against the glossy white half-panelling. Even now, Mel could not believe the luxury of carpeted stairs, which made no clattering noise as she went up.

Above, the new wallpaper with the tiny yellow flowers shone cheerfully. The stairwell had been unbelievably difficult to re-paper, and in the end she had asked Mr Miller to come to the rescue. He had shown her how to put boards across stepladders, but she still could not reach, and he had put up the two longest pieces for her.

Her own bedroom she had painted with the remains of the yellow emulsion paint, but, aside from cleaning, she had not touched her mother's bedroom. Something had kept her back. When her mother was settled they would plan it together. Make it really pretty and luxurious.

The downstairs front room was the most successful, Mel thought, wandering in. A Victorian parlour now. Cleaned, the carpet had come up a rich dark green with pink roses, and the pale apple-green walls were exactly the right colour to go with it. This afternoon the whole room was shining, bathed in sunlight. The pink loose cover of the sofa looked very professional, hiding the torn upholstery.

The curtains had been difficult. The old lace curtain, dark yellow with dirt, had fallen apart completely when Mel had taken it down to wash. There had been no side curtains, and Mel could not afford any more of the pink linen. In the end she had used one of the red velvet curtains from their house in Lothian, which were at the bottom of the packing case. There had been large picture windows in the Lothian house, and the curtains had been long and wide. Mel cut one in half and Saira's mother had machined it into the right size for her. It was a waste really, but why keep them? They were never going back to Scotland, and they looked very rich next to her polished desk gleaming in the alcove. In the other alcove was the bamboo stand, full of plants. A small oval mirror she had found in one of the cupboards hung over the mantelpiece, reflecting the sauce boat trailing tradescantia. In the fireplace, the iron grate was glossy and black and growing a deep pink geranium, donated by Mrs Martin as a welcome-home present.

The green velvet armchair was here too, newly cleaned with upholstery shampoo, and the stain on the arm had gone.

She looked through into the other room. It had been a marvellous idea, having the doors taken away. Everything looked so much more spacious.

Through the opening she saw the polished floor and the pine table and chairs. It still gave her a thrill to see the floor's golden smoothness. She remembered the hours of sanding and varnishing and shuddered. It had been the worst job of all. In front of the fire was the sheepskin rug from the packing case.

On the table, filled with apples and looking good, was her wobbly pottery bowl, the only one to emerge unscathed from the kiln in her four weeks of pottery.

There were glass shelves over the cupboards in the alcoves, now, with glasses and some of the china from the second packing case. There was space, too, for a television, if her mother wanted to hire one. On the walls were some old Victorian flower prints which she had found in the junk shop and framed herself, with some of the old frames.

But the curtains had been a problem here too. They had been a dirty shade of beige, with an ugly purplish-red flower. Mel giggled, remembering how she had dumped them into a gold dye bath. They had come out mottled an even odder shade of mustard with brown flowers. But now, hung against the yellow emulsion and the pine wood, they looked quite good.

The kitchen had taken a lot of courage. It was dominated by the pine dresser with its shining brass handles, and Mitch's sink cupboard matched it beautifully. She remembered the despair of finding the horrible yellow stains, ruining the new paper—but even this had turned out for the best. Thinking all the time she must be crazy, Mel had painted the walls a dark chocolate brown to cover all the stains, and then, greatly daring, had painted the old worn lino with dark brown lino paint. She painted everything else white—the woodwork, the doors, the old kitchen table. The overall effect was either going to look hideous and dark or smart and modern.

As she looked round now she heaved a sigh of relief. It looked smart and modern, and you hardly noticed the old cooker, which remained blackened and discoloured, no matter how much it was cleaned. Mel wished she'd had enough courage to paint that too.

She had even managed to give the lavatory outside a new coat of paint, and put down a piece of the green carpet left over from the stairs.

Hours of hard work, Mel thought. Ten months of her life, she realised suddenly. But somehow it had all been worth it. She had learned so much. She had proved to herself that she was capable and could do jobs they said girls couldn't do. When she left school she would do some bricklaying classes or some plumbing, and maybe, if the Development Association was successful, build a bathroom extension, like Joe.

There was a car drawing up outside. Mel flew to the door and tugged it open.

Her mother was standing on the pavement looking along the road, stunned. A thin man with a kind expression and fine floppy hair, was getting a suitcase out of the boot.

Mel hovered on the doorstep, awkward, suddenly not knowing what to do. She took a step forward and made herself hug her mother. There was no response, only the dazed look in her mother's eyes, focusing on her. "Mel?"

A thin, stone-cold curl of alarm spiralled up Mel's spine. That dazed look . . . Surely it wasn't going to start all over again?

Her mother was wearing the turquoise dress Mel had bought for her and shoes with high heels. Her hair had been cut and blow-dried into a smooth curved style. She looked so young and pretty. Mel had forgotten how pretty she was.

"It's all different. Painted. And you're different too," her

189

mother said. "You're taller and plumper and your hair—it's so different."

Mel relaxed and laughed. "You look different too!"

Her mother, remembering, suddenly stood aside. "This is Peter. I want you to be friends. He drove me from the hospital. He's a friend of mine."

Mel smiled at him, and tucked her arm into her mother's. "Come and see what I've done to the house. It's a surprise for you. I've been working on it ever since you went into the hospital."

She opened the door wider and, with a little cry, her mother brushed past, staring at the passage and staircase. Then she walked into the front room. Mel saw that the dazed look was back. Her mother moved slowly around staring at the objects and furniture.

"Lots of people have helped," said Mel, happily. "But I did most of it myself. I've been working Saturdays to get money to pay for things."

Her mother did not reply. Mel glanced at Peter. He smiled at her reassuringly. "It looks very comfortable and cosy."

Her mother, silent, agitated, walked quickly along to the kitchen, and then, hardly stopping, came into the living room through the other door, and stood, staring around wildly—at the floor, at the pine table, at the light, opened-out space.

Peter was watching her, puzzled and alarmed. Mel pushed away the curling apprehension and said, trying to hold her excitement, "You are wondering about that terrible old sideboard. I swapped it for that armchair. The table and chairs only cost five pounds! Do you remember what it used to be like in here?"

It was as though her words broke the spell. Her mother spun round, her face contorted. Her eyes were wide and her cheeks ashen. "What have you *done*, you wicked girl? What have you done to my little house?"

190

For a disbelieving moment, Mel stared at her. She looked at Peter, speechless, her hands moving in appeal.

"Marian, love," he moved forward, quickly.

"It's all gone! What have you done, you evil, wicked girl? I could kill . . ." Her mother's voice rose to a croaking scream before being muffled against Peter's jacket as he caught her hands and pulled her to him.

Mel's stomach moved violently with remembered fear and disgust. A vision of the stinking room and the heaped boxes spun before her eyes. It was all going to start again. The dirt, the degradation, the beatings.

She stumbled into the kitchen and seized a plastic carrier bag, and with mounting hysteria, raced up the stairs. In her room she grabbed her few clothes from hangers and drawers, stuffing them wildly into the bag. A towel, toothbrush, washing things, shoulder bag, jacket . . . and she was out of the house, her feet flying of their own accord down the street. She must get away. Never go back. Never go back to that fear and horror. Not again . . . She turned the corner, taking great gulps of air, and then another corner, and reaching a patch of waste ground, vomited violently.

Afterwards she walked, not knowing where, or for how long.

When it was quite dark, she found she was in a street with a familiar name and realised that she was outside Keith Edwards' flat. It was the ground floor of an elegant terrace house with steps up to the front door and a portico. There was a light in the window, but the curtains had been drawn.

Mel felt the tears sliding down her cheeks with relief. Keith would know what she should do. He had made her promise to come to him if she was in difficulties. She had thought, proudly and stupidly, that she would never call on him for help, but now the relief of knowing that there was someone to look after her was so overwhelming she had to sit down on one of the steps until she could get a grip on herself.

After a while, she got up and pressed the lighted bell above his name.

Twenty-three

"All right," said Lou, the following evening when she walked into the hospital late. "You look bloody awful. Out with it."

"She came home. She hates what I've done to the house, the decorating—everything. It was all a waste of time." She stared, unseeing, at the shining floor. She did not want to cry now. She felt frozen inside, and sledgehammered with lack of sleep and too much emotion.

"And?"

"I walked out. I hope you don't mind—I spent the night at the shop, on the sofa."

"You look done in."

"I've been at school all day and I stayed to help put up decorations for the school disco tomorrow." She laughed grimly.

Lou did not speak, still waiting. At last she looked at him. "That's it."

"There's more. Spit it out."

There was another silence. She tried to speak, swallowed, and suddenly burst out, "It's Keith, my teacher."

"Oh, that one," Lou grunted disparagingly. "I heard about him from Mitch."

Mel gave a short laugh, cold and ugly. "Yes, you're right. *That* one. The one I was crazy about. *Stupid*, that's me. I really believed it, when he said he'd do anything to help. Made me promise I'd see him if I had problems. I ought to have known when he didn't bother about me at Christmas.

After I walked out I was . . . well, I was very upset, crying, and I felt ill. I wandered about. Didn't know what to do. Then I went round to his flat."

"And he said, 'Come back later, I'm busy.' "

Mel stared at him. "How did you know? Who told you?"

"No one. It happens to everyone at some time. You're not the only one."

"He said, 'Surely it's not that urgent.' He said, 'Can't you manage . . .' " Her voice choked.

"He probably had a female there."

"He did," said Mel, dully. "It looked like Dee Tracey."

Lou began to roll a cigarette. "There you are then. Couldn't very well invite you in."

Mel looked up, white. "He didn't care about my trouble, Lou. Why did they pretend to care about what happened to me? You should have heard the way they went on at me about Mitch at school. Shitty hypocrites!"

"Watch the language. I'm not one of your foul-mouthed generation."

"I'll go," said Mel stiffly, and got up.

"Now don't you get on your high horse. You know I speak out. What you come here for if you don't want straight talking?"

Mel sat down again, tired. "I don't know. I just wanted to tell someone. I can't cope any more."

"You've coped on your own till now. What are you going to do?"

Mel shrugged. "Don't know. Don't care. I'm finished. For a while I really thought you could control things. Get things done. I even began to think that maybe you could trust people. But it's all a con."

Lou scratched his chin thoughtfully, watching her. His whiskers made a rasping sound. "You went to Keith Edwards. Why didn't you go to Mitch?"

"*Mitch?*" She stared at him blankly, at a loss.

194

"You know where he lives, don't you?"

A slow, dark colour climbed up her cheeks and she looked away. "Why would I go to Mitch? We've had a row anyway."

"You're supposed to be engaged," Lou said sharply. "You're messing that boy about."

She was exasperated. "I keep telling you—it was a joke —and not my joke either. Anyway, he would probably have a girl in his bed too!"

She saw that Lou was twisting his face as though he had found a fly in his beer. She turned round quickly. Mitch was standing behind her, furious.

"As it happens, you're *wrong*," he said, icily. "I haven't been to bed at all. I've been looking for *you*. I got back last evening and called round to see you and you'd gone. What kind of stupid game are you playing?"

Mel stiffened. Lou coughed and said, "Mitch . . ."

"Your mother is frantic. You'll have to go back."

Mel turned her shoulder. She said to Lou, "When I think of all the work I did in that place, I must have been stark raving mad. I worked most evenings. All day in the holidays. They couldn't believe it at school when they saw the 'before' photographs in my project. Everybody thought it was marvellous what I'd done on hardly any money. I wanted to give her a good place to come back to, a real home. I suppose I was waiting for her to say, 'It's wonderful' or 'It's lovely' or 'What a beautiful surprise'." She looked at Mitch fiercely. "You know what she did? She turned on me shrieking like a mad witch. 'I'll kill you. What have you done to my little house?' *My little house!* That filthy, stinking dump. I couldn't believe it."

"She says she didn't mean it, Mel. She's sorry. She says it was the shock of seeing it all so different."

"I'm never going back. I couldn't live there again. Not after that . . ." Her voice stopped abruptly and she looked away, swallowing rapidly. "You don't understand what it was like before. I can't go back."

"Just see her, Mel. She's so upset. You'll put her back in the hospital."

"I don't care. Why should I? I did my best, my very best, and it was no good. She threw it back in my face. Rejected me again. What about my feelings?"

"I'll go with you. It won't be so bad."

"No. You don't know what you're talking about. I don't know what it's got to do with you anyway."

He was angry. "I'm a friend, aren't I? I was looking for you all night and most of today, Mel. Where were you?"

"Walking. Then I went to Keith's flat and . . ."

"So that's it! I might have known." Mitch was angrier than she had ever seen him before. "I should have guessed, but I didn't think even you would be *that* stupid."

"What are you talking about?" Mel stood up and faced him, hostile.

"I suppose you've been there most nights, since I stopped seeing you. He's using you, Mel. That kind of bloke—you're just another fast lay to him. He doesn't care about you or love you. You don't mean anything to him."

She laughed briefly, hurting and angry. "You're right. The story of my life in a nutshell. Nobody cares. Nobody loves me. And you know all about fast lays, don't you?"

He went even paler. "What's that supposed to mean?"

"You know."

"It wasn't like that."

"You could have fooled me."

"You're so bloody young and stupid, you don't understand a thing."

"No, I don't. That's true. I don't know why you're in such a bad temper for a start. I didn't ask you to stay up all night and come looking for me. I take care of myself. Better than anyone else. Keep out of my business."

196

"That's right," he said, bitterly. "You've spelled it out often enough. Not my business. I thought we were friends but you run to him with your trouble. Stay all night. Okay, Mel, don't worry. I've got the message at last. It's taken a time, but it's got through now. Not *my* business. Malc can phone the papers and say the engagement is off."

"It was never on," Mel said, impatiently.

He looked at her for a moment, his eyes suddenly too bright. "For me it was. I thought you might like it enough to make it permanent. You must have known I wasn't using you to get rid of Roxy."

He waited for her reply, but Mel just stared at him, dumb and incredulous.

"It was a mad idea. Okay Mel, don't worry, I'll stay out of your life in future." He hesitated a few more seconds, waiting, then when she stood silent and unmoving, he turned on his heel and pushed out through the swing doors.

Mel looked after him, her anger drained away, too tired and exhausted with emotion to stop him. "I didn't know, Lou. I never even imagined . . ."

"Well," said Lou, disgusted, "I hope you're pleased. You're doing very well, pulling everything down. Why didn't you tell him you were at the shop and not with this Keith?"

She shrugged, sullen. "If he thinks I'm screwing around, let him."

"Where are you going to stay tonight?"

She shook her head, staring at the floor.

"All right, I'll tell you what you're going to do. You're going back to Cowcross Street."

"No."

"Yes you are. I've got a deal for you. If you go back and sort out the trouble with your mum, you can have the flat above the shop. In fact, you can have the lease of the shop and run it for yourself if you like."

"You're joking." She saw that he was grinning at her like a crocodile.

"I've got some good news, Mel. It'll even cheer you up."

"You're getting out of here."

"Well, yes, that as well. But listen, girl, we've hit the big one."

"The big one?"

"The jackpot. The one gamblers like me dream about."

"You mean, you've won some money?"

"You and me both. Remember the Christmas money? Well, I never had that much spare cash out of the blue before, so I kept it to put on an accumulator."

Mel felt faint. "You mean you put all our Christmas takings—two-hundred and fifty-nine pounds fifteen pence —on a *horse*?"

"Six horses. An accumulator. Six winners in six races."

Mel felt the ward tip around her. She sat down on the chair quickly. "I have got it right? You put all the money, mine as well as yours, on six horses that *all* had to win on the same day?"

He grinned. "I always swore I'd hit that bastard one day. All the money he's had off me."

"I thought you didn't swear," Mel said, coldly. "I think you must be mad. *Six* horses."

"Thirty thousand pounds."

Mel took a deep breath. "None of your other bets ever came up before. He'll refuse to pay. He'll run away . . ."

"What a bloody pessimist you are. You'd stop a hyena laughing."

"I don't believe any of this. Lou, are you telling me that you could actually put fifteen thousand pounds in my hand *now*?"

Lou averted his eyes. "Well, not exactly, Mel. I've, er, invested it for you along with my share."

Mel took another deep breath. "Not another accumulator?"

"I've invested it in Syd's betting shop. That's how I know he won't run away, see?"

Mel laughed. She laughed until the tears ran down her cheeks and laughed some more, until the Ward sister began to look at her over her glasses. Lou was indignant.

"That's a nice little investment, don't you worry. He has some very tidy profits does Syd. No one ever beats the bookmaker, my girl. I've always wanted to be a bookmaker."

"But why are you giving up the shop? You said it was your independence, that you needed it to keep you going. Where are you going to live?"

"Ah, that was the problem. I'll never get up them stairs at the shop again, Mel. Not with this gammy leg. I'm going in with Syd. He's got a nice little bungalow behind the business. Very snug. No stairs. Two minutes to the betting shop. Five minutes to the boozer. Meals on wheels. Home Help. I reckon I could go on for another twenty years and die a millionaire."

Mel started to laugh again, and found she was crying at the same time.

"I'll give you a tip about Life, my girl. I don't give tips often, so listen. Always be ready for change and ride with it. It's more interesting and it's more comfortable. Only a fool tries to block change. Now then, when are you going back to see your mum? I want to get all the business sorted out."

Mel stopped laughing. "I'm sorry, Lou. *I can't.* Not tonight. I'm too frightened. I've got to think about it first."

"All right then. Stay in the shop tonight. But bring your mother in here soon. I want to get the business transferred all legal and tidy, and we need your mother's signature because you're under age."

Twenty-four

Outside the hospital it was already dusk. Mel had turned towards Market Street before she realised she was making her way home automatically. She stopped dead in the middle of the pavement, and a small figure, sobbing helplessly, bounced off her. Winded, she clutched his arm and found herself staring at a familiar dark face.

"Stevie Miller! What on earth's the matter?"

He was a tough little boy, not given to crying. "It's Ben. The Police have got him. They've taken him off somewhere. I don't know where. I came to try to find mum at the hospital. Dad's on a late job down in Surrey and Lucinda's gone to some meeting with Joe. I don't know what to do. Ben hasn't done anything. He just come from school and we was delivering some leaflets for the Development Association and he was going to buy me some fish and chips . . ."

"Never mind about the fish and chips!" She shook him impatiently and he started to cry again. "*Listen.* You go into that door, there, to the reception desk. Say there's an emergency at home and can you see your mum. Tell her I've gone to the police to see what's happening. Right?"

He nodded, gulping, and Mel, not waiting another second, took to her heels and sped along the pavement.

By the time she got to the police station in the High Street she was so angry she hardly had time to feel frightened at being in a police station for the first time in her life.

"I'm looking for a friend of mine," she said to the man on

the desk. "They said he'd been brought in . . ." At that moment she caught sight of Ben, slumped on the bench opposite the desk, his arms folded, his legs sticking out.

"Oh, there you are. What's happened? What are you doing here? I met Stevie."

"You know this boy?" asked the desk sergeant.

"He's Ben Miller."

The young policeman standing next to the sergeant looked sceptical. "They all look alike. How do you know it's him?"

Mel gaped at him. "Of course it's Ben Miller. He's a friend. I've got a room in his house. He goes to my school. His sister Lucinda is my best friend. Who else would it be?" She understood suddenly. She said, sarcastically, "I can recognize her too. And his mother and father. And his married sister and his married sister's husband and their two children . . ."

Ben was grinning. "Wicked!"

"Of course I recognise him. I don't wear glasses. Or blinkers."

The desk sergeant was looking worried. He said to the younger man, "You sure this was the kid?"

"He was standing about with a friend at the corner of Hereward Street and Market Street at six o'clock. Later I saw them leaving Cranshaw Super Market by the back entrance . . ."

"All right."

Mel smacked the desk impatiently. "That can't be true. Ben was at school with me at six o'clock, with Bernard Wilson, Tom Kerrigan and Conny Ravopolous. We've been doing decorations for the school disco tomorrow. He was still there when I left about seven to go to the hospital. He couldn't have been in Hereward Street at six."

"I suppose the lot of you will say he was there all evening?" sneered the young policeman.

"That's where he was—and there's loads of us who saw

him. He couldn't have been anywhere else at six or seven o'clock either."

The older policeman was looking far more worried now. "Well, we can get it all sorted out in the morning."

"Look," Mel tried to hold on to the remains of her temper. "Why should Ben spend a night here, because that, that . . . person . . ." her finger twitched at the young policeman, "made a mistake?"

"Now then, young lady . . ."

"Ben's mother will be really mad when she gets home from the hospital. It's not fair."

"You go along home now."

"Look, I'll get Bernard or Tom. They'll tell you . . ."

"They probably made it all up outside the station," sneered the young policeman.

Mel drew a deep breath. "If you won't believe me or my friends, perhaps you'll believe some of the teachers who were there. I'll get someone."

She marched angrily out of the station.

The older policeman was annoyed now. "They probably all go to William Watt. The Headmaster is a right sod. We've had it all before. If she gets him out of his house at this time of night, he'll have your ears. Mr Thomas doesn't like policemen."

The young policeman was red round the neck. "I tell you . . ."

"I heard. I also heard you say they all look alike to you. You're in the wrong job for that kind of statement. Better start thinking really hard about your future."

Mel, outside the police station, was desperately trying not to panic. She must get someone as quickly as possible before they could charge Ben and everything got out of hand. Which teachers had been there at school? For a moment her mind was blank, and then she remembered Mrs Green counting out cans of *Seven Up*; Mr Biggs, testing the sound system; the schoolkeeper; Mr Thomas, the Headmaster; Keith Edwards, in charge of the decorations.

Mr Thomas would be best but he lived way out in Essex. She could ring Directory Enquiries to get his number. Or Mrs Green had given her a telephone number to ring in an emergency—and she would know Mr Thomas' number too . . .

She was trying not to think of the obvious and quickest choice. Keith Edwards—only just around the corner. He could be there in minutes. There *must* be somebody else other than Keith. How could she go to his flat again?

Mel hesitated, feeling hot all over, a sick feeling in her stomach. She knew she really had no choice. This was more important than personal feelings. Speed was essential. She had to put her pride in her pocket. Ben was in real trouble. Keith Edwards would see that this was really important. He would want to help Ben. She started down the road.

A thin, rock-strong, brown hand gripped her arm and swung her round. The small group of older Black boys closed round her, dangerous, threatening.

"Where's Ben Miller? What's happening?"

She recognised Winston Reynolds from Sylvan Street and Johnston Gates from Blossom Bank, who had both left school two years ago and had been out of work ever since. She had seen some of the other boys hanging round the market at lunch times.

"Let me go, Winston, I'm in a hurry."

"We heard stories. *Where's Ben?*"

"With the police. They think he's done a job at Cranshaw's. Now let me go, I tell you I've got to get help."

He loosened his grip. "I thought he was doing disco stuff at school tonight."

"He was. But then he went out to deliver the Development Association leaflets and the police got him. They've made a mistake, but they won't listen to me. I've got to get Keith Edwards. They'll believe *him* . . ."

A boy laughed. "He be busy, man. He won't turn out late for we."

Mel jerked herself free. "Don't be stupid. Ben can't stay there all night. He didn't do it. Get out of my way."

The boys moved back and huddled together.

"It's true then."

"It's not fair."

"We treated like dirt."

"Nothing we can do."

And Winston's soft voice, "We'll get him out."

Feeling frightened and apprehensive, Mel set off at a run. There had been a lot of tension between the local boys and the police recently, a succession of nasty small incidents. It could easily blow up into something big.

There was a light on in Keith's flat, but although she pressed the bell urgently several times, there was no reply. He *must* be there. The main door was slightly open. She walked in quickly and banged on his door. Sorry to spoil your fun, she thought grimly, but this is a lot more important.

Suddenly Keith's door flew open. He had a towel round his waist and he was dripping wet and furious.

"What on earth was all that banging?" He stopped, staring at her.

She swallowed. "I'm sorry to disturb you, Sir. It's really urgent and the door was open . . ."

He stepped back grimly. "Come in. What do you want again?"

"Something awful's happened."

"It'd better be a major disaster, getting me out of the shower."

"I'm sorry. I didn't want to come but . . ."

"You know Mel, it's really too bad. I only just got away from that bloody school and the bloody decorations and here

204

I am being pestered again. Don't you think I'm entitled to just a little private life?"

Mel was white. "You told me to come to you if I needed help. You made me promise."

"You were here last night too. It's getting a habit, isn't it? I'm getting sick of it."

"Please, Keith, it's Ben Miller. You've got to come."

"Ben Miller!" he exploded. "I've had enough of him tonight. He's a bloody nuisance. Larking about, disturbing every . . ."

Mel shouted desperately, "He's been arrested!"

He looked at her, exasperated, not understanding. "Wait there, I'll get some clothes on." He disappeared into his bathroom.

Mel looked around the room, wishing he would hurry up, conscious of the valuable minutes ticking away. Just as Keith came back, zipping his jeans and pulling a sweatshirt over his head, the door behind her opened and a girl let herself into the room with her own key.

For a moment the scene fixed itself. The girl looked at him, then looked at Mel, her mouth tightening.

"No wonder you're always late for dates with me. Got your timetable wrong, darling?"

"Now listen, Carol . . ."

"She's a bit young, isn't she? But no, I can see she's got what you like."

Mel said, "I'm one of his pupils."

"Spare me the sordid details," she drawled. "You've played around once too often, Keith Edwards. I've had enough. The engagement is OFF." She turned and walked out, slamming the door.

Keith swung on Mel furiously. "I hope you're satisfied. That was the girl I was hoping to marry. Listen, and listen good. I don't want you coming round here all the time. You're ruining my social life. What's so urgent you can't see

205

me at school? Just because I kissed you once there's no reason to keep pestering me."

The terrible injustice of it all stung her, but underneath she was hurting more than she had believed possible. Hadn't she learned *yet* that it was stupid to trust people and ask them for help?

She said carefully, forcing out the words. "I've only been here once before—when I really needed help, and you told me to go away. But this time it's not for me. There is bad trouble and it's going to get worse, unless something is done quick. I thought you might be able to stop it, but you're no good. You know, I really believed you?" She laughed and mimicked him, "Call on me for anything, any time. *You can rely on me.*" She laughed again and opened the door.

"Okay, cut the dramatics," he said annoyed, "What . . . ?"

"Don't bother, I'll ring Mr Thomas instead. He's a proper teacher." She slammed the door hard.

Keith switched on the television. He sat in front of it for an hour, seething. Then he thought of Mrs Green and decided it would be a good idea to check out Mel's story, just in case it was more than adolescent hysteria. There couldn't be anything seriously wrong, could there?

Mr Thomas was already driving back from his Essex suburb, using swearwords he had picked up from his pupils. Just wait till he got his hands on that fool, Edwards. He thought, with grim satisfaction, that it was a good thing he had not yet sent off his report on Keith Edwards' probationary year. Edwards would find it very difficult getting another job by the time he had finished with him. Mr Thomas looked at his watch and put his foot down on the accelerator.

The word had run like petrol fire through the streets that Ben Miller had been nicked. Everyone knew that he had been putting up decorations at school and delivering Association leaflets. The injustice of it made everyone angry. Ben was very popular in the school and well-liked in the neighbourhood since his part in the litter campaign. A menacing crowd of boys, mostly Black with a few whites, gathered outside the police station, demanding that Ben should be released, and refused to disperse when told to do so. After an exchange of insults with the young policeman, Winston Reynolds was arrested. The angry crowd went berserk, throwing stones at the police station, and running down the High Street, smashing shop windows and leaving a trail of devastation behind them.

By the time Mr Thomas arrived, it was too late. Fifteen of his boys had been arrested and charged with affray, a much more serious charge than disturbing the peace. They would be lucky to stay out of prison.

Appalled, Keith Edwards got the story from Mrs Miller herself. Most of the people in Cowcross Street were standing at their doors, shouting news to each other anxiously. Mr Singh had gone down to the police station to bail Ben out, and other people were trying to calm Mr Miller, who had just got home from work and was so angry he looked as though he would tear the police station apart with his bare hands.

Mel was there with Joe and Lucinda, who was crying. Keith put his hand on Mel's shoulder and she shrugged it off with loathing. "Go away, Mr Edwards. This is your fault. You could have stopped it happening. There are a lot of people very angry with you, including Mr Miller there. And Mr Thomas is waiting for you at the police station." She laughed. "He was being very rude about you."

"Mel . . ."

She said, softly, "Don't ever talk to me again, Mr Edwards."

She would have walked away, but her mother darted across the road and caught her hand. "Mel, please don't go away. Not yet."

Mel felt the familiar sick fear rise in her stomach. "Where's Peter?"

"He's gone with Mr Singh in case any of the boys have been injured. He's a male nurse. Please come in for a few minutes, Mel. I must talk to you. Make you understand."

Mel hesitated, hostile. "All right. But only until we know what's happened to Ben."

She stood stiffly against the pine table, watching her mother walk nervously up and down the room.

"I don't want to talk about what happened here when I was ill."

"No, I didn't think you would," Mel said, bitterly.

"I want to talk about yesterday. That was terrible. I want to say I'm sorry."

"So am I," said Mel. "A pity you didn't stop to think a bit before you started screaming at me again."

Marian Calder said, desperate, "Please listen, Mel. You don't understand how it is when you have a breakdown. Please God you won't ever know. You want to get well, but a part of you doesn't, because if you do you'll have to start living again. Taking up all the old problems and the old pain, and you know you won't be able to cope with them.

"So although I was better, I'd kept a little secret place in my mind. I thought I could always come back here if things got rough. My little dark hole to hide in and everything would go away again. Nothing to worry about."

"Like you did before," said Mel, uncompromisingly.

Her mother looked away. "Peter didn't want me to come back here. He knew the danger. He's a good man, Mel. He wants to marry me."

"Was he another patient in the hospital?" Mel asked, stonily.

208

"No, although I suppose anybody who would want to marry me would seem crazy to you. He's a male nurse. We met at the Hospital Dance."

"That's nice." Mel moved towards the door. "I think I'll be going."

"Please stay, Mel."

"I can't live here any more. I can hardly stand being in the place."

"I'm sorry I spoiled it for you. You've worked so hard and it's beautiful. I never dreamed one of these houses could look like this. And the road is different too. When I saw it—all I could think of was that you'd taken away my little dark bolt hole. I *had* to start again. I was so angry. But Peter talked to me and explained. And then, later, I went upstairs to my bedroom."

"But I didn't touch your bedroom. I just cleaned it."

"I know. It was like looking into a nightmare. It brought it all back. The dirt, the misery. I remembered exactly how it was. Mel, I don't *ever* want to go back to that again. I know that now. With Peter's help and the tablets they gave me, I think I will be all right. I really think I'm well. You've helped a lot. What you did in this house. The dark bolt hole is gone forever. A new beginning.

"Mel, what can I say? I know I must have hurt you badly. Mrs Martin told me how hard you have worked. Every night for months. Saturdays at the shop to help pay for all the new things."

"You can have everything except the desk—that's mine," said Mel. "It's special to me."

Her mother looked around. "I just can't believe . . . I suppose I feel jealous and guilty too. You've done all this by yourself."

"I had help," said Mel. "Mr Miller, Mitch, Saira next door. Saira's mum made the curtains."

"And I didn't do anything. I brought you here. I could

have made the place nice, but I just let it all go. You showed me what I ought to have done."

Mel said, cautiously, "You were trying to earn a living. You were too tired . . ."

Her mother shook her head slowly. "I was angry. Resentful. I thought there ought to be someone to look after me. I even blamed your father for dying. I felt it wasn't fair. All the other women had a man to look after them. I knew I couldn't look after myself."

Mel stared at her, remembering her own feelings the year before. Someone to look after her. "I felt that too," she said, slowly. "But there wasn't anyone. I realised you have to look after yourself."

Somehow the tension between them had relaxed. Marian Calder made tea in the kitchen.

"This kitchen is so different. You've got a real flair for decorating, Mel."

"I hope so. I've applied for a full-time course in interior design in September," said Mel. "Keith . . . At school they think I could get in."

"Yes," said her mother, pleased. "That's good. I think we could manage. Peter might help. And there would be grants and . . ."

Mel laughed. She pulled herself on to the kitchen table. "You won't believe this, but Lou—Mitch's grandad—made a bet on a horse for me. Six horses. And they won. I've got a share in a betting shop. He *says* we're going to be rich. And he's offered to sign over the lease of the junk shop to me."

"But Mel, can you manage a shop like that by yourself? I mean, you're only a girl and young too . . ."

"I'm nearly eighteen, and I've been running it since November," said Mel, coldly. "The shop has been going very well. I've been making a profit. You'll have to sign the papers for me though, Lou says."

"Of course I will, if you want that. It sounds a splendid opportunity."

Mel said, hesitating, "I'm going to keep my room at Mrs Miller's and decorate the flat above the shop to live in. I don't want to come back here. I feel free now. I've got used to being free."

"Mel, you're my daughter. I'm grateful to Mrs Miller, but surely . . ."

Mel stared at the floor. "I know what you're going to say. But it's not just what happened when you came home yesterday. It's all the months, *years*, when you were sick. I'm frightened of you. I don't trust you any more. I don't trust anybody much. I don't know how much I can love you."

"I've always loved you, Mel, even though it didn't seem like it." She sounded hurt, hopeless.

Unexpectedly Mel felt a sudden rush of pity. Suddenly she wanted to cry. Who could you blame for mental illness? She said, slowly, "If you want, I'll call in some evenings. I'm willing to . . . try . . . to start again."

Twenty-five

Soon after Mr Thomas arrived at the police station Ben was released without a charge. The fifteen supporters were bailed out by Mr Singh and went home, subdued, to face their angry parents. Mr Thomas got home at two o'clock in the morning, and sat down immediately, to enjoy himself drafting his report on Keith Edwards.

The next day after school Mel found Lucinda and Ben still depressed and upset.

"The important thing is that Ben's been cleared—that's good news, isn't it?" Mel protested.

"It's all right, but what about the others? None of them can afford to pay the fines. They'll all go to gaol. *Boys are so stupid!*"

Mel said, "Maybe Lou would let me sell my share of the betting shop and then I could . . ."

They stopped eating to stare at her. "Are you crazy?" said Lucinda.

"Well, I feel guilty. If I could have got someone there quicker, I might . . ."

"You know as well as I do nothing ever stops that Winston Reynolds when he goes on the rampage. Remember the gym windows? Remember those chairs he threw down the library stairs?"

"All right," said Mel. "I know you're trying to make me feel okay, but I still feel bad about it. Can't we raise some money for the fines? We had the litter campaign and we've set up the Development Association."

Lucinda said, sarcastically, "Oh yes! A nice little jumble sale? There are fifteen of them, Mel. Mr Singh says the fines will be heavy. And there are the damages and the legal fees. It'll cost thousands!"

"All right," said Mel, angrily. "We'll just sit back and let them all go to prison. Even a jumble sale would be better than nothing."

"We need to think," said Lucinda. "There must be some way of getting our hands on real money."

"Football pools," said Ben. "Professional boxing. Darts. Snooker. Golf. Tennis. Bestseller. Pop song in the charts."

"That's it!" screamed Lucinda, sending Ben's fish pie down the wrong way.

"Write a pop song?" said Mel. "What kind of loony . . ."

"We'll put on a concert."

Mel started to laugh. "At the municipal theatre."

"That's right," said Lucinda, not laughing. "It seats two thousand people."

"It also costs five hundred to hire."

"Two thousand seats at say, a fiver each, that's ten thousand pounds less five hundred. Plus sale of programmes, badges, refreshments, tee shirts . . ."

"Who is going to pay five pounds for a seat? Who are you going to get to play your concert? It costs the earth to get a good band."

"Not me. *You.* You're going to ask Mitch Hamilton. We could fill the theatre twice over if Assassination played a benefit."

"*No,*" said Mel, the laughter wiped away.

"It's the only answer."

"No! He finished with me, Lucinda. I'm not asking Mitch for anything. I'm not asking *anybody* for anything. I've had enough of giving people a chance to wipe their feet on me."

"Mitch isn't Keith."

"Ask him yourself."

"It's you he's crazy about."

"That's more than I know. I won't do it."

"You're just as bad as Keith Edwards," Lucinda said, bitterly. "You say you want to help, but you won't even do just a little thing. It doesn't matter to you that all those families will be in bad trouble for years, trying to repay the money they'll have to borrow to keep their boys out of gaol. You don't really care."

Mel said, suddenly hard and angry, "Why *should* I care? Nobody looked after me when I was in trouble. Nobody bothered when my mother was beating me up and screaming mad. They all knew, but they didn't do a thing. No one helped *me*. They all rejected me. Even you, Lucinda."

"My mother cared," said Ben. "She helped you. Got the ambulance. Went up to the school for you. Gave you a room in our house."

Mel's eyes filled with tears.

"You know," said Lucinda, "you're getting a really big chip on your shoulder, Mel. If you're not careful you'll get all twisted and bitter inside—too proud to let anyone close to you in case they hurt you."

"Proud! That's a good one, coming from you, Lucinda, *princess*. You're so full of good advice, it's a pity you don't take some yourself."

"I have," said Lucinda, smugly. "I'm leaving the boutique in September."

Mel gaped at her. "Leaving! But what about your modelling?"

"I've decided to go to the college to get my A levels and try for university. I'm going to do Economics and Political Theory. I want to know how things got this way. So what's wrong, dummy?"

Mel grinned. "It's the shock. I won't say I told you so."

"I made up my mind yesterday. It was the trouble about Ben, of course, and Joe, partly. He convinced me. I'm going to try to get into politics. We need some Black women in Parliament. Joe says it's a waste of time—Parliament, that is. But I think we've got to start somewhere. Mind you . . ." she was grinning, "I don't see why I shouldn't make some extra cash modelling for a while. There's nothing wrong with good clothes and a decent house, but Joe's right. It wouldn't be enough for me." Her grin widened. "I might even be the first Black woman Prime Minister. How does that grab you?"

"You couldn't do worse than the white ones," Mel said, morosely. "But you're not Prime Minister yet, and I'm still not asking Mitch."

"It's not for yourself. It's for the boys."

"I don't know how to get hold of him anyway. He won't come to the shop any more. He doesn't want to see me."

"That's no problem," said Lucinda. "I've got his phone number. I'll ask him to call round."

"How come *you* have his phone number?"

Lucinda grinned. "You're jealous! So you do like him."

Mel flushed and turned away.

"Did *you* ever ask him for his phone number, Mel?"

"No, of course not. Why should I?"

"He wanted you to ask, Mel. He was dying for you to ring him. He left it with me in case there was an emergency and you needed help. He's worried about you."

Mel laughed shakily.

"Please, Mel, ask him. We can't let things go on like this. You know what I mean. All this hate has to stop sometime. We have to do something."

Mel hesitated, looking at the carpet. "I know what you mean." There was a long silence. At last she said, "Yes. You're right. We have to do something ourselves."

But on Saturday morning, when Mitch walked into the shop her resolution faltered. He was white and hostile, looking at her like a stranger.

"Lucinda said you wanted to see me."

"I . . ."

"She said there was something important."

What had he imagined? Did he think . . . ? She stood up. "N-not about us," she managed to say.

He smiled, tightly. "I didn't think so. Well, go on. I haven't got all day. Barney's waiting outside in the car."

Her heart sank. "It's difficult . . ." She swallowed. "I want . . . Will you . . . I want to ask a favour."

He waited. She swallowed again, and forced the words out one by one. "I need some help."

"Why don't you ask your dear old teacher, the lovely Keith Edwards? You're nothing to do with me."

Mel felt a sharp pain in her chest. She drew in a long deep breath, and walked away into the back room.

"*Mel* . . ." Mitch came after her and turned her head with his hands. "Oh, bloody hell! Look, I didn't mean to hurt you. I'm just so angry and jealous and miserable, I'm not thinking straight. Tell me what you want."

Mel rubbed her wet face with the back of her hand.

"There's nothing to be jealous about."

"When you go sleeping with another guy? When you run to him with your troubles and keep pushing me away?"

"I haven't been with Keith. I went round to him, it's true. I thought he would help with my mother, but he had someone else there. He told me to clear off. I came back here to the shop, in case my mother went looking for me at Mrs Miller's. I slept on the sofa and went to school next day. You can ask Lou."

"I see." Mitch's face was stony. "So nothing has changed. You're still waiting in line till he gets around to you."

Mel said, "I was a fool. I'm never going to speak to him

again." The pain pushed through her control. "I thought he was a good person who cared about people. Lucinda warned me. I feel so stupid."

She told him about Ben and the riot at the police station and the way Keith had refused to come. "If we'd got there straight away, Ben would have been let out and the other boys would have gone home. Now there's all this trouble and they can't pay the fines and damages and they'll go to gaol and get police records. It could ruin their lives."

"Barney and I heard about the trouble on the news and talked about Assassination playing a benefit concert for them. If you like I'll tell Malc to fix it up. We can fit it in before the world tour."

"That's what I was going to ask you!"

"I know Paul Devlin and Chris Carter of Easy Connection. Maybe they'd do a personal appearance. That would draw more people in."

"Oh Mitch! You are kind." Mel flung her arms around him and hugged him tightly. "You're like Mrs Miller. You don't just talk. You *do* something. I didn't think you would help after the way I treated you."

He held on to her, his face buried in her neck. He was shaking and Mel felt a sudden wetness on her skin, but boys didn't cry did they?

"I thought it was all over between us." His voice was muffled. His arms tightened painfully. "I love you so much. I don't care who you were thinking of that night, it was me you were loving with your body, Mel."

She kissed his cheek and then, as he turned his head, his mouth.

"I loved being with you Mitch, but I thought you just wanted a girl to play around with when you were passing through. I was just ordinary, so I knew I mustn't let myself get serious about you. You know what musicians are like."

"Labels," said Mitch.

217

"I didn't want to chance being hurt again. Somebody else turning away, rejecting me. Keith seemed so kind and good. He was big and fair-haired like my dad and I thought . . . I'd be safe with him."

"You're pretty good at rejecting people yourself, Mel."

She stared at him.

"You've been rejecting *me* for a long time. You didn't want my help, my interest, my love. You kept me at a distance. Not because of anything I did. You just gave me a label 'pop star' and switched off. I'm not like that, Mel. I'm fed up and lonely. I've always been lonely. I've always wanted a girl like you and a family to take care of.

"I used to look out for you, last year, when you passed the shop. You looked so alone too. I couldn't believe my luck when you came into the shop."

Mel turned away and looked out of the window, remembering. "I was having a bad time. You know, I tried to kill myself."

He gripped her arm painfully. "What did you say?"

"It was when I began to realise I was alone. That nobody was going to look after me and I'd have to do it myself. I couldn't face it. I was going to fall in front of a tube train. I sat on the wall and waited, but when it came, my hands pushed me away."

Mitch let out a long breath; he was shaking again. "Mel, don't ever . . . *Promise* . . . It'd kill me too."

"No, I wouldn't try again. Now I think you have to see it through. The funny thing is that when I was waiting for somebody to start looking after me, nobody wanted to know. I could have died quite easily. But when I began to look after myself, I found I wasn't alone at all. All sorts of people tried to help. But I've been hurt so much it's difficult for me to trust people. I keep getting let down."

He held her so close to him that she could feel his heart beating, and kissed her and kissed her again.

She put her arms around his neck. "You're lovely."

"You still haven't said it, Mel."

"I—I do love you Mitch. It was growing all the time but I wouldn't let myself realise it. I was too afraid."

"Do you trust me, Mel? Enough to marry me when you've finished your college course?"

Mel hesitated. It felt like she was about to jump into the open-air swimming pool on a cold day. Could she find the courage to try one more time?

She took a long, deep breath. "Yes, I trust you, Mitch. There's a lot of things I wanted to do, though, before . . ." She took another deep breath. "Okay, let's get engaged. When you come back from your world tour. I'd really like that."

"Thank Christ for that!" said Barney's voice from the door. He was leaning, interested, against the frame. "He's been bloody impossible lately. You'll be all right with Mitch, Mel. He's got some funny ideas, mind . . ."

"Thanks, friend," said Mitch, wearily. "Why don't you bug off, Barney? We don't need company."

"Great. No problem," said Barney, "but first I've got a question."

"GO AWAY BARNEY!"

"Can I be bridesmaid?"